A VERY
SCALZI
CHRISTMAS

JOHN SCALZI

SUBTERRANEAN PRESS 2019

First Edition

ISBN
978-1-59606-932-9

See pages 143-144 for individual story credits.

Subterranean Press
PO Box 190106
Burton, MI 48519

subterraneanpress.com

Manufactured in the United States of America

To Natalie Metzger, whose illustrations for this, and for my previous story collection *Miniatures*, are total delights, and have made the books so much better than they would be otherwise.

Also to everyone who keeps Christmas, however they choose to do that.

TABLE OF
CONTENTS

9   Ho Ho Intro, or, the Reason for the Season(al Collection)

13   Science Fictional Thanksgiving Grace

17   A Bitter November

21   The 10 Least Successful Holiday Specials of All Time

29   An Interview with Santa's Lawyer

39   A Personal Top 10 of Things That Are Not Titles to Christmas Songs and/or Lifetime Holiday Movies and Honestly I Don't Understand Why

41   Christmas in July

65   Interview with Santa's Reindeer Wrangler

73   8 Things You Didn't Know You Didn't Know about Your Favorite Holiday Music

81   Jackie Jones and Melrose Mandy

87   An Interview with the Christmas Bunny

95   Jangle the Elf Grants Wishes

101   Script Notes on The Birth of Jesus

107   Sarah's Sister

129   An Interview with the Nativity Innkeeper

137   Resolutions for the New Year: A Bullet Point List

HO HO INTRO, OR, THE REASON FOR THE SEASON(AL COLLECTION)

I really like Christmas.

Yes, yes, I know. What a brave and controversial statement! It's not like Christmastime has taken ten percent of the annual calendar in the US, from the moment the plates are cleared from Thanksgiving dinner to the last second of the New Year's Day Bowl games, or that there are entire cable channels that by this point could air nothing but their own Christmas movies non-stop from January to December. It's not as if the day is so important in our culture and our own economy that it has its own financial gravity well, around which the fortunes of small business all over the world orbit. And, of course, it's not as if it's meant to celebrate the birthday of the founder of a religion billions of people across the globe celebrate and follow.

Even so! Christmas makes me happy. And strangely enough—or perhaps not—it makes me happier the older I get. I enjoyed it as a kid, because, well. Who doesn't like presents. But as I've gotten older I've learned to appreciate everything *else* about it. The *feeling* of the season, as it were. The traditions and the idea that, at the end of the year, we try for a little kindness and generosity. These things are worth celebrating and carrying forward into the rest of the calendar.

Also, and relevantly for what you're reading now, Christmas (and the holidays on either side of it) gives me something to write about and have fun with on an annual basis, both for the audience on my own personal site, and for audiences elsewhere. As much as I love Christmas, I also love taking some of the traditions of the season and either highlighting their built-in absurdities, or introducing a few absurdities of my own. These explorations of Christmas have become a thing I look forward to annually, and I'm delighted that I now get to put them into a stocking-sized collection for you to enjoy as well.

And what can you expect? Well, most of the pieces in this collection are short (usually less than two thousand words long). Some of them are "interviews" with people who have something to do with a somewhat obscure aspect of Christmas (this is how you'll meet Santa's lawyer, for example), and others of them are "informational" articles about things like Christmas songs or TV shows (note that "informational" is in quotes for a reason). Most of these pieces involve Christmas, but a couple involve Thanksgiving or the

New Year. Because I am best known as a science fiction writer, at least a couple of the pieces are specifically science fiction-themed. You'll know because they feature dinosaurs and robot uprisings.

That said, there are some holiday curveballs in here too. There's at least one Christmas-themed poem, and two full-fledged Christmas stories, at least one of which I wrote with the specific intent of making my mother-in-law tear up. See if you can guess which one it is.

Finally, three of the pieces, "Christmas in July," "Jangle the Elf Grants Wishes" and "Resolutions for the New Year," are new and exclusive to this collection. You get to be the first anywhere to see them. I had fun writing them, so I hope you have fun reading them.

Truth to be told, I had fun writing all of the pieces in this collection. I think it's accurate to say that the book you hold in your hand is, piece for piece, the one that contains the most joy I've had writing than any other. That's saying something. I hope it comes through.

Merry Christmas (even if it's not Christmas when you pick this up), and a happy new read to you.

John Scalzi
May 6, 2019

SCIENCE FICTIONAL
THANKSGIVING
GRACE

Dear Great and Gracious Lord,

This Thanksgiving, we pause to reflect on all the bounty and good fortune with which you have graced us this year. Thank you, Lord, for this feast we have in front of us and for the family and friends who are with us today to enjoy this bounty and this day with us, even our Cousin Chet. Thank you for our health and for our happiness.

We also thank you for the world and that in your wisdom you have not stopped the Earth's core from rotating, collapsing our planet's magnetic field and causing microwaves from the sun to fry whole cities, requiring a plucky band of scientists to drill down through the mantle and start the core's rotation with nuclear bombs. That seems like a lot of work, so we are pleased you've kept the Earth's core as it is.

We also thank you for once again not allowing our technology to gain sentience, to launch our own missiles at us, to send a robot back in time to kill the mother of the human resistance, to enslave us all, and finally to use our bodies as batteries. That doesn't even make sense from an energy-management point of view, Lord, and you'd think the robots would know that. But in your wisdom, you haven't made it an issue yet, so thank you.

Additionally, let us extend our gratitude that this was not the year that you allowed the alien armadas to attack, to rapaciously steal our natural resources, and to feed on us, obliging us to make a last-ditch effort to infect their computers with a virus, rely on microbes to give them a nasty cold, or moisten them vigorously in the hope that they are water-soluble. I think I speak for all of us when I say that moistening aliens was not on the agenda for any of us at this table. Thank you, Lord, for sparing us that duty.

Our further thanks to you, our Lord, for not allowing the aliens to invade one at a time and conquer us by taking us over on an individual basis. That you in your wisdom have not allowed aliens to quietly inhabit our bodies and identities—the better to attack us by cornering us in the rec room or outside while having a smoke—means that we can enjoy each other's company without undue paranoia. It also means that if we are obliged to set a flame thrower on Cousin Chet, as we are sometimes tempted to, we will not see his flaming head sprout arms and try to scurry away. And for that we are truly blessed.

Thank you for not allowing the total moral and economic decline of the United States, our Lord, that would turn one or more of our great cities into a prison or spring any number of apocalyptic scenarios upon us that would turn our planet into a vasty wasteland where only dune buggies and leather-clad miscreants have survived. It's not that we have anything against leather-clad miscreants—I refer you, Lord, to the previously mentioned Cousin Chet—but we prefer them to be in the minority, and also those dune buggies so rarely have seat belts—that's just not safe.

Most specifically, thank you, Lord, for not sending a large meteor or comet tumbling straight at the planet, forcing the government to turn to oil-rig operators to save us all. That oil rig in the Gulf this year didn't exactly inspire confidence, if you know what I mean, Lord. And while we know that humanity would likely survive such a massive impact thanks to those underground cities the government has built, we are not at all confident that any of us at this table would get a pass into those cities, and we don't have either dune buggies or wardrobes made mostly of animal hide. So thank you, Lord, for not making us worry about that this year.

Finally, Lord, thank you for once again keeping the scientists from bioengineering dinosaurs back to life. While the idea of a pterodactyl with stuffing and all the trimmings seems like a good one at first blush, getting past the raptors in the supermarket parking lot would probably be a challenge, and we would end up having to stake one of our own to the shopping-cart return so the rest of us could get past, and I'm not sure that we could persuade Cousin Chet to do that more than once.

For these and so many other things, Lord, we offer our humble gratitude to you this Thanksgiving. However, I think I speak for everyone when I say we would still like speeder bikes, so if you could get someone to invent those by Christmas we would all be obliged. Amen.

A BITTER
NOVEMBER

Me (going into the kitchen and finding someone going through the fridge): Who's there?

Strange Yet Oddly Familiar Person: It's *me*, you idiot.

Me (peering to get a better look): …November? Is that you? What are you doing here?

November: Eating some of your leftovers. (Holds up Tupperware) Mind if I finish off your cranberry sauce?

Me: No, that's fine. What I meant to say is that I thought you had already left.

November: What's the date?

Me: Uh…November 29.

November: Right. I still have today and tomorrow, you know.

Me: I suppose you do.

November: Damn *right* I do. I have thirty days. Every year. It's not like I'm *February*. (Sits, sullenly, to eat his leftovers.)

Me: I know. It's just that after Thanksgiving, it feels like November should be over, you know?

November (bitterly): You think I don't *know* that? You think I don't know that as soon as people wrap foil over the turkey pickings and shove them in the ice box, they start looking at me like I missed some sort of important social cue? They start looking at the closet my jacket is in and then down at their wrists as if to say, *whoa, look at the time.*

Me: I'm sure they don't mean anything by it.

November: And nobody actually wears wristwatches anymore! They all get their time from their cell phones. That's what makes it *extra demeaning*.

Me: I don't think everyone wants you out the door on Thursday evening. There's Black Friday, after all.

November (rolls eyes): Oh, *right*. The "traditional start of holiday retail." *Holiday retail*, dude. "Holiday" is just *code*, you know. For *December*.

Me: Code?

November: Friggin' December, man. He was always pushy, you know. Always so *entitled*. Mr. "Oh, I have *two* major religious holidays every year." Yeah, well, you know what? Some years, I have Diwali. Okay? *That's* a festival of lights, too. A billion people celebrate it. And that's just the Hindus! I'm not even counting the Jains or the Sikhs!

Me: I think that those cranberries might have fermented on you.

November: Don't patronize *me*, buddy. All I'm saying is December is not *all that*. *I've* got election day. *I've* got Veteran's Day. *I've* got Thanksgiving. *I'm* the All-American month.

Me (as my cell phone buzzes): Hold on, I'm getting a text.

November: Who is it?

Me: It's July. The text says, "I felt a great disturbance in the Force, as if November was whining about something and was suddenly silenced BY AMERICA'S BIRTHDAY."

November (holds up hands): You see? You see what I have to put up with?

(DOOR OPENS. DECEMBER bustles through, carrying packages)

December: Oh, man! You wouldn't believe what kind of madness is out there in the stores these days. People are really getting into the holiday— Oh. November. Sorry, I didn't see you there.

November: Of course you didn't. God forbid you should acknowledge my *existence*, December.

December (to me): Did I come at a bad time?

Me: We're having a bit of a moment, yes.

December: I can come back.

November: Yeah, in *three days,* you usurping bastard!

December: I'll just go now.

(December leaves)

November: That's right! Go! And take your crappy Christmas carols with you! (Breaks down weeping)

Me: Aw, come on, November. Don't be like that.

November: I just want people to appreciate me, okay? For my entire stay. Is that too much to ask?

Me: No, I suppose it isn't. I'm sorry, November. It was wrong of me.

November (sniffling): It's all right. I know you weren't trying to offend me. Anyway. I'll just be going now. (Gets up)

Me: No, November. Sit down. Please. You can stay if you want.

November: Yeah? Really?

Me: Of course you can. You can even help me with some stuff around the house, if you want.

November (narrows eyes): You're about to put up Christmas decorations, aren't you.

Me (guiltily): Of course not.

THE 10 LEAST SUCCESSFUL
HOLIDAY SPECIALS
OF ALL TIME

An Algonquin Round Table Christmas (1927)

Alexander Woollcott, Franklin Pierce Adams, George Kaufman, Robert Benchley and Dorothy Parker were the stars of this 1927 NBC Red radio network special, one of the earliest Christmas specials ever performed. Unfortunately the principals, lured to the table for an unusual evening gathering by the promise of free drinks and pierogies, appeared unaware they were live and on the air, avoiding witty seasonal banter to concentrate on trashing absent Round Tabler Edna Ferber's latest novel, *Mother Knows Best,* and complaining, in progressively drunken fashion, about their lack of sex lives. Seasonal material of a sort finally appears in the 23rd minute when Dorothy Parker, already on her fifth drink, can be heard to remark, "one more of these and I'll be sliding down Santa's chimney." The feed was cut shortly thereafter. NBC Red's 1928 holiday special "Christmas with the Fitzgeralds" was similarly unsuccessful.

The Mercury Theatre on the Air Presents the Assassination of Saint Nicholas (1938)

LISTENERS OF radio's Columbia Broadcasting System who tuned in to hear a Christmas Eve rendition of Charles Dickens' *A Christmas Carol* were shocked when they heard what appeared to be a newscast from the north pole, reporting that Santa's Workshop had been overrun in a blitzkrieg by Finnish proxies of the Nazi German government. The newscast, a hoax created by 20-something wunderkind Orson Welles as a seasonal allegory about the spread of Fascism in Europe, was so successful that few listeners stayed to listen until the end, when St. Nick emerged from the smoking ruins of his workshop to deliver a rousing call to action against the authoritarian tide and to urge peace on Earth, good will toward men and expound on the joys of a hot cup of Mercury Theatre on the Air's sponsor Campbell's soup. Instead, tens of thousands of New York City children mobbed the Macy's Department Store on 34th, long presumed to be Santa's New York embassy, and sang Christmas carols in wee, sobbing tones. Only a midnight appearance of New York mayor Fiorello LaGuardia in full Santa getup quelled the agitated tykes. Welles, now a hunted man on the Eastern seaboard, decamped for Hollywood shortly thereafter.

Ayn Rand's A Selfish Christmas (1951)

IN THIS hour-long radio drama, Santa struggles with the increasing demands of providing gifts for millions of spoiled, ungrateful brats across the world, until a single elf, in the engineering department of his workshop, convinces Santa to go on strike. The special ends with the entropic collapse of the civilization of takers and the spectacle of children trudging across the bitterly cold, dark tundra to offer Santa cash for his services, acknowledging at last that his genius makes the gifts—and therefore Christmas—possible. Prior to broadcast, Mutual Broadcast System executives raised objections to the radio play, noting that 56 minutes of the hour-long broadcast went to a philosophical manifesto by the elf and of the four remaining minutes, three went to a love scene between Santa and the cold, practical Mrs. Claus that was rendered into radio through the use of grunts and the shattering of several dozen whiskey tumblers. In later letters, Rand sneeringly described these executives as "anti-life."

The Lost Star Trek Christmas Episode: "A Most Illogical Holiday" (1968)

MR. SPOCK, with his pointy ears, is hailed as a messiah on a wintry world where elves toil for a mysterious master, revealed to be Santa just prior to the first commercial break. Santa, enraged, kills Ensign Jones and attacks the *Enterprise* in his sleigh. As Scotty works to keep the power flowing to the shields, Kirk and Bones infiltrate

Santa's headquarters. With the help of the comely and lonely Mrs. Claus, Kirk is led to the heart of the workshop, where he learns the truth: Santa is himself a pawn to a master computer, whose initial program is based on an ancient book of children's Christmas tales. Kirk engages the master computer in a battle of wits, demanding the computer explain how it is physically possible for Santa to deliver gifts to all the children in the universe in a single night. The master computer, confronted with this computational anomaly, self-destructs; Santa, freed from mental enslavement, releases the elves and begins a new, democratic society. Back on the ship, Bones and Spock bicker about the meaning of Christmas, an argument which ends when Scotty appears on the bridge with egg nog made with Romulan Ale.

Filmed during the series' run, this episode was never shown on network television and was offered in syndication only once, in 1975. *Star Trek* fans hint the episode was later personally destroyed by Gene Roddenberry. Rumor suggests Harlan Ellison may have written the original script; asked about the episode at 1978's IguanaCon II science fiction convention, however, Ellison described the episode as "a quiescently glistening cherem of pus."

Bob & Carol & Ted & Santa (1973)

THIS ABC Christmas special featured Santa as a happy-go-lucky swinger who comically wades into the marital bed of two neurotic '70s couples, and also the music of the Carpenters. It was screened for television critics but shelved by the network when the critics, assembled at ABC's New York offices, rose as one to strangle the producers at the post-viewing interview. Joel Siegel would later write, "When Santa did his striptease for Carol while Karen Carpenter sang 'Top of the World' and peered through an open window, we all looked at each other and knew that we television critics, of all people, had been called upon to defend Western Civilization. We dared not fail."

A Muppet Christmas with Zbigniew Brzezinski (1978)

A YEAR before their rather more successful Christmas pairing with John Denver, the Muppets joined Carter Administration National Security Advisor Brzezinski for an evening of fun, song, and anticommunist rhetoric. While those who remember the show recall the pairing of Brzezinski and Miss Piggy for a duet of "Winter Wonderland" as winsomely enchanting, the scenes where the NSA head explains the true meaning of Christmas to an assemblage of Muppets dressed as Afghani mujahideen was incongruous and disturbing even then. Washington rumor, unsupported by any Carter administration member, suggests that President Carter had this Christmas special on a repeating loop while he drafted his infamous "Malaise" speech.

The Village People in Can't Stop the Christmas Music—On Ice! (1980)

UNDETERRED BY the miserable flop of the movie *Can't Stop the Music!,* last place television network NBC aired this special, in which music group the Village People mobilize to save Christmas after Santa Claus (Paul Lynde) experiences a hernia. Thus follows several musical sequences—on ice!—where the Village People move Santa's Workshop to Christopher Street, enlist their friends to become elves with an adapted version of their hit "In The Navy," and draft film co-star Steve Guttenberg to become the new Santa in a sequence which involves stripping the future *Police Academy* star to his shorts, shaving and oiling his chest, and outfitting him in fur-trimmed red briefs and crimson leathers to a disco version of "O Come All Ye Faithful." Peggy Fleming, Shields and Yarnell and Lorna Luft co-star.

Interestingly, there is no reliable data regarding the ratings for this show, as the Nielsen diaries for this week were accidentally consumed by fire. Show producers estimate that one in ten Americans tuned in to at least part of the show, but more conservative estimates place the audience at no more than two or three percent, tops.

A Canadian Christmas with David Cronenberg (1986)

FACED WITH Canadian content requirements but no new programming, the Canadian Broadcasting Company turned to Canadian director David Cronenberg, hot off his success with *Scanners* and *The Fly,* to fill the seasonal gap. In this 90-minute event, Santa (Michael Ironside) makes an emergency landing in the Northwest Territories, where he is exposed to a previously unknown virus after being attacked by a violent moose. The virus causes Santa to develop both a large, tooth-bearing orifice in his belly and a lustful hunger for human flesh, which he sates by graphically devouring Canadian celebrities Bryan Adams, Dan Aykroyd and Gordie Howe on national television. Music by Neil Young.

Noam Chomsky:
Deconstructing Christmas (1998)

THIS PBS/WGBH special featured linguist and social commentator Chomsky sitting at a desk, explaining how the development of the commercial Christmas season directly relates to the loss of individual freedoms in the United States and the subjugation of indigenous people in southeast Asia. Despite a rave review by *Z* magazine, musical guest Zach de la Rocha and the concession by Chomsky to wear a seasonal hat for a younger demographic appeal, this is known to be the least requested Christmas special ever made.

Christmas with the Nuge (2002)

SPURRED BY the success of *The Osbournes* on sister network MTV, cable network VH1 contracted zany hard rocker Ted Nugent to help create a "reality" Christmas special. Nugent responded with a special that features the Motor City Madman bowhunting, and then making jerky from, four calling birds, three French hens, two turtle doves, and a partridge in a pear tree, all specially flown in to Nugent's Michigan compound for the occasion. In the second half of the hour-long special, Nugent heckles vegetarian Night Ranger/Damn Yankees bassist Jack Blades into consuming three strips of dove jerky. Fearing the inevitable PETA protest, and boycotts from Moby and Pam Anderson, VH1 never aired the special, which is available solely by special order at the Nuge Store on TedNugent.com.

AN INTERVIEW WITH
SANTA'S LAWYER

Please state your name and occupation.

My name is Marta Pittman, and I'm a partner at Xavier, Masham, Abbott and Stevens.

And you're Santa Claus' lawyer.

That is correct. More accurately, I'm the partner in charge of our firm's Seasonal Litigation and Clearances practice, which has as a client NicolasNorth LLC, Santa's corporate entity.

I wasn't aware that Santa needed to have his own corporation.

Of course he does. One, Santa heads a massive global enterprise, whose activities are spread over a wide range of areas. Having a corporate structure allows him a measure of organization and systematization. Two, Santa has a large number of employees, mostly elves, who have their own idiosyncratic employment issues and practices. The corporate structure simplifies hiring, benefits, and negotiation of labor disputes. Three, due to the nature of Santa's work, he has immense exposure to liability. The corporate structure acts as a shield for Santa's personal wealth and property.

Santa has liability issues?

Tons.

Can you give an example?

Obviously I can't speak about current cases under litigation, but let me give a general example. As you know, a common way for Santa to enter single-unit dwellings is through a chimney.

I always thought that was artistic license.

No, it's correct. Santa is usually entering from above and the chimney is the most direct route. "Quick in, quick out" is the keyword here. The important thing is, this point of Santa egress is well-known. And every year, immediately after Christmas, dozens of suits are filed against Santa, claiming property damage caused by Santa entering and leaving through the chimney. The usual allegation is that Santa's body shape was a predicate cause.

Because he has a round belly that shakes like a bowl full of jelly.

Which is not true, by the way. I've seen Santa out of uniform. That dude is ripped.

He is?

Absolutely. Delivering packages to millions of children in a single night is a heck of workout. The thing is, people don't know that, and so they file these fraudulent suits predicated on what they assume about Santa's weight, based on his marketing.

I assume most of these suits get dismissed.

Usually with prejudice. And also the plaintiffs go onto Santa's "naughty" list for the next year. Santa takes a dim view of fat shaming, especially for fraudulent purposes. But the point is, since Santa is operating as NicolasNorth LLC, even if one of these suits was successful, Santa wouldn't lose his house.

At the North Pole.

It's actually in Sarasota, Florida.

That's…disillusioning.

It was on our advice. Anchoring a home on rapidly-dwindling polar ice is risky from an insurance standpoint.

And Santa's Workshop?

Also not on the polar ice. Technically in Nunavut. We recently negotiated a 99-year lease near Cape Columbia. Which brings us to another aspect of our firm's services for Santa: International law.

Right, because Santa delivers presents all around the world.

Yes, he does. And up until 2013 he had to negotiate clearances and flight paths with every single country on the globe. People think Santa works one day a year and then sits on the beach the rest of the time. In fact until recently he spent most of his non-Christmas time in meetings with mid-level bureaucrats, trying to make sure the toys he was delivering weren't subject to import restrictions.

That doesn't sound especially jolly.

It's good if you're racking up frequent flyer miles. But Santa flies his own aircraft, so he wasn't even getting that.

What happened in 2013?

My firm negotiated a rider to the Bali Package at the Ninth Ministerial Conference of the World Trade Organization. As of December 7, 2013, Santa has automatic clearances in every WTO signatory state. Cut his annual paperwork 95%.

So *now* Santa gets to spend time on the beach.

There's a reason he lives in Sarasota.

You mentioned elves before.

What about them?

What special employment issues do they have?

Well, before I get to that, I should state unequivocally that Santa is an equal opportunity employer, and seeks to create a diverse and welcoming work place for everyone at NicolasNorth LLC and all its subsidiaries and affiliates. He obeys all Canadian employment laws and requires all his sub-contractors and suppliers to adhere to the highest ethical business standards and practices.

That's a very specific disclaimer.

There have been unfounded rumors of unfair employment and labor practices at NicolasNorth LLC by some of Santa's business rivals.

Business rivals?

Let's just say that someone whose name rhymes with "Leff Gezos" is going to be getting coal in his stocking until the end of time. And not, like, the good kind of coal. We're talking the crappiest sort of lignite that's out there.

All right, noted.

With everything above taken as read, the thing about elves is that they're not actually human, so most labor and employment laws don't apply to them.

If elves don't qualify as human under the law, what are they?

Under Canadian law, they're technically animals.

Animals.

Yes. Just like reindeer. And technically, under Canadian law, Santa's Workshop qualifies as a federally inspected farm, the oversight of which is handled by Canadian Food Inspection Agency.

So, *technically*, Santa's elves have as many rights as veal.

I'm offended at this comparison, and also, yes.

Okay, so, that feels icky in a whole lot of ways. Maybe Leff Gezos was on to something.

It's obviously not optimal from the public relations point of view.

Now I'm imagining tiny elves in jaunty caps, making toys in crates.

It's not like that.

Convince me.

Well, among other things, Santa's Workshop is a union shop.

Really.

Yes. Affiliated with the Canadian Union of Postal Workers.

Postal workers?

The CUPW is a serious union. You cross them, they'll mess you up.

And the CUPW doesn't mind that the elves technically aren't human.

The elves pay their dues like anyone else. They're good.

Santa's okay with a union shop?

Santa believes in the dignity of labor, and wishes to avoid any potential elf uprisings.

That's…good to know.

Seriously, elves are vicious. They look adorable, but get on their bad side just once and they. Will. *Cut.* You.

I'll remember.

You better.

What other legal issues do you help Santa with?

Well, one major issue—probably the biggest issue, really—is policing Santa's intellectual property.

Santa has IP?

Or course Santa has IP. In a larger, existential sense, it could be said that at his root, Santa is nothing *but* IP.

I always assumed Santa was in the public domain.

It's a common misconception. In fact NicolasNorth LLC is the repository of numerous trade and service marks which we are obliged by law to vigorously defend.

So, Santa's red suit—

The red suit device is trademarked.

And the red cap—

Covered as part of the red suit device and also legally its own trademark. So's the beard, before you ask.

And the sleigh—

The sleigh and eight of the reindeer and also all of their names, trademarked.

Not Rudolph?

The issue of Rudolph is a matter of ongoing litigation and I can't comment on it at this time.

You're suing over Rudolph?

I'm sorry, I really can't comment.

But—

Look, do you want coal this year? Because you're heading that direction.

Sorry.

Let's move on.

You say you have to defend Santa's intellectual property, but I see red suits and beards everywhere.

Clearly it's in Santa's interest to have his trademarks be ubiquitous.

But if people are using your trademarks for free, aren't you at risk for losing them?

Who said they're using them for free?

They're not?

Absolutely not. NicolasNorth LLC gets a licensing fee for every red suit you see.

How much?

It's a sliding scale, based on several factors, including business income, charitable status, intended use of the trademark, and whether the person who is wearing the suit intends to be naughty or nice in it.

People are naughty in a Santa suit?

Some people are. Santa doesn't judge people for their kinks, but he does expect them to pay for them.

And people pay without complaint.

Most do. Some don't. Which is why Santa retains us.

And if they're still balky after they talk to you?

We send in the elves.

One more question, if you don't mind.

Not at all.

Santa is well known for making a list, and checking it twice.

For the purposes of appropriate gift distribution, yes.

It does raise questions of how Santa gathers that information in the first place.

I'm not sure what you mean.

I mean the idea of Santa as an all-knowing arbiter of right and wrong, knowing when someone is sleeping or awake and so on. Some might say that's both judge-y and creepy.

Only the people who want coal in their stocking.

Well, see, that sounds like a threat right there.

I don't see *how*, but all right. Let's say that there were legitimate concerns about Santa's methods. First, I would remind people that Santa's services are *opt in*; you choose whether to have Santa part of your seasonal holiday experience.

I don't remember opting in.

Well, you probably didn't. But your parents did, on your behalf. And when they did, part of the user agreement was that Santa—which currently legally means NicolasNorth LLC—is allowed to collect data from various sources in order to make a determination of your gift worthiness, using what we in the industry call the "N/N Matrix", a multi-dimensional tool using constantly updated algorithms for a precise and accurate placing of each person on the gifting spectrum.

That sounds complicated and not great, from a privacy standpoint.

I can assure you that NicolasNorth LLC does not share your information with third parties.

How does Santa collect this information in the first place?

In the old days, kids would write letters to Santa, and we also had strategically placed employees to personally evaluate children.

Spies?

Mall Santas.

But malls are failing left and right these days.

They are, and kids don't send letters to Santa as often anymore. Those information avenues are closing. Fortunately Santa foresaw this problem, and made some key moves to assure a vast new data source.

The CIA.

Jeez, no. Talk about liability issues! And remember, this is supposed to be opt in. Fortunately there's a place people go these days to voluntarily expose every aspect of their lives in a wildly promiscuous manner the CIA could previously only dream of.

Oh, God, you're talking about Facebook.

Six percent owned by NicolasNorth LLC, by the way.

You're saying Santa Claus is a tech billionaire.

Like I said, Santa made some key moves. And it wasn't like he wasn't a billionaire before.

What do you mean?

Where do you think Santa gets all that coal?

Santa is a *coal baron?*

He's divested. Mostly. Our advice. Again, liability issues.

I'm still unsettled at the idea Santa is data mining my social media posts.

He's legally allowed to. It's right there in the user agreement.

I didn't read the user agreement.

No one reads the user agreement. Doesn't mean it's not there.

Any final advice for people wanting to stay on Santa's good side, legally speaking?

Pay your Santa suit license fees, drop hints about what your kids want for Christmas in your Facebook posts, and don't blame Santa if you have a pokey chimney, that's just basic home maintenance. And be good, for goodness' sake.

And what about you? Have you been bad or good this year?

I mean, I'm a lawyer.

Point taken.

It's fine. I could use the coal.

A PERSONAL TOP 10 OF THINGS THAT ARE NOT TITLES TO CHRISTMAS SONGS AND/OR LIFETIME HOLIDAY MOVIES AND HONESTLY I DON'T UNDERSTAND WHY

10. A Colonoscopy for Christmas

9. If Reindeer Can Fly Then How Did Daddy Hit One with His Truck

8. Christmas on Reddit

7. I've Got the "My Family Has Left Me and All I've Got to Get Me Through the Holidays Is Coors Light and a DVD of *Die Hard* Set to Repeat" Blues Again, Mama

6. Jingle! Jangle! Gerbils!

5. What Do You Mean I Missed Hanukkah Again, There Are Eight Goddamn Nights of It

4. A Child's Christmas on XBox

3. Officer I Didn't Mean to Kick His Teeth In, but He Said "Happy Holidays" Instead of "Merry Christmas"

2. Mama, Why Does Santa Need My Kidney?

1. Mansplaining Christmas to Mary

CHRISTMAS
IN JULY

It was the kids who woke him, of course, with their excited squeals and their urging for their parents to get up, please, please *please*, so they could start unwrapping the gifts. Kerry was six and was the main instigator of the pleadings, as she was in most things, while Damie, almost four, held back quietly, occasionally echoing his sister's urgings but mostly letting her run point.

"Come on, Dad," Kerry pleaded. "Get up."

Tim Collier looked over at the alarm clock on the bed stand, which read 6:30 a.m., and then put his head back down on the pillow. "Why are you even *up*," he murmured to his daughter. "It's a Saturday." Kerry was many things, but a voluntarily early riser was not one of them. School days were an exercise in prying her out of her bed. Tim, who was the same when it came to early rising, then and now, could sympathize. Which was why, at this moment, he was grumpy about his kid, standing at the side of his bed.

"It's not Saturday, it's *Christmas*," Kerry said.

"Christmas!" Damie echoed.

Tim looked over to his children, and then over to Evie, his wife, who was just emerging out of her own cocoon of sleep. "Apparently, it's Christmas," he said to Evie.

"Oh, good, I like Christmas," Evie said, then rolled over to get back to sleep.

"Mom!" Kerry protested. Damie offered a squeak.

"It's too *early* for Christmas," Evie said, from the other side of her pillow. She was better at getting out of bed on most days than Tim, but not on Saturdays, which she considered her "I get to sleep in" day.

"But *presents*." Kerry went up on her tiptoes as she said this. Damie watched and seemed to consider doing the same, but his balance was not great on the best of days. He stayed flat on his feet.

"I'm going back to sleep now," Evie said. She hiked up the blankets around her shoulder, which was her Saturday morning symbol for "all dispute is now ended under penalty of death."

Kerry, sensing her mother was no longer persuadable, turned back to her father. "Can we have our stockings?" The general rule was that stockings could be opened without parental supervision, but actual presents needed an adult to police all the wrapping paper.

"Knock yourself out," Tim said, and his children squealed in happiness and scampered from the room and raced down the stairs toward the Collier's fireplace, which wasn't really a fireplace because an electric heater with a blower and fake LED flames over a bed of artificial glowing coals isn't actually a fire. But "electric heater place" wouldn't look as good on a real estate flyer. And it did have a mantel, so there you are. Tim went back to sleep without thinking any further on the conversation he'd just had with his children.

Roughly an hour later Tim and Evie had gotten enough sleep, and, after considering and then rejecting the idea of agreeably sleepy morning sex on the grounds that the children were already up and running around the house, both of the adult Colliers hauled themselves out of bed, put on robes and debated whether coffee first and then brushing teeth, or brushing teeth and then coffee. Coffee first was agreed upon. Tim and Evie padded down the stairs and then turned the corner to the kitchen, which thanks to the open floor plan flowed into the living room, which was a riot of Christmas decorations. A massive tree, almost to the ceiling, stood in the corner. The pile of gifts underneath was enormous. Kerry and Damie, the detritus of their stockings all around them, were watching the television, where adorable animated creatures were singing about the true meaning of Christmas.

Tim and Evie stared at the holiday overload in their living room. Evie was the first to speak.

"Where the actual hell did all *this* come from?" she said.

It was July 18.

Kerry turned her attention from the TV and looked at her parents, eyes bright with joy. "Can we open the presents *now?*" she asked.

"**DID YOU** freak out?" Colonel Arthur Barker asked Major Tim Collier, as they strode the halls of the Pentagon an hour and a half later. They were on their way to an emergency briefing.

"No," Tim said. "Not on the outside, anyway. I didn't want to let Kerry or Damie think there was anything wrong. As far as they knew, it was Christmas."

"They didn't think anything about it being July."

"They're six and three," Tim pointed out.

Barker nodded. "Fair point."

"What about your kids?" Tim asked Barker.

Barker smiled tightly. "Well, mine are seventeen, fifteen and twelve. They figured out something was off pretty quickly."

"What did they think?"

"They thought I was pranking them," Barker said. "And then Lindsey thought I was doing it to one-up Veronica and her new husband. She thought I was acting out because her mom married a millionaire. I had to remind her I was too cheap for that." They turned into their conference room and, as aides to two of the generals sitting at the long table in the center of the room, took seats at the periphery. Tim's boss, General Mavis Dunwoody, turned her head to acknowledge his presence. Normally he would have accompanied her into the room. But today was a messy day for everyone.

Two minutes later they stood as the Secretary of Defense stepped in to the room. Evan Kells did a perfunctory wave, motioning everyone to sit, and then sat at the head of the table and looked around. "The President woke up to a White House filled with Christmas trees and holiday spangles that neither she nor her staff put up, and she was not at all happy about that. I have to brief her on the military implications of this in exactly half an hour, so someone tell me what the hell is going on."

"Christmas is going on," said General Chuck Hibbens.

"Which would be great if it weren't July," Kells said. "But because it is, and because whoever is causing it can get into one of the most secure homes in the world and set up entire hallways of Christmas decorations without either the security cameras or the Secret Service catching them, I'm a little concerned about the implications of this event. So someone tell me something. Anything. Now."

Hibbens nodded to his aide, Colonel Margie Gomez, who stood and opened up a folder. "As far as we can tell, this is happening globally. At some point near six a.m. Washington time, presents, Christmas trees, decorations and holiday food just…showed up in people's houses."

"Into every house on the planet?" Kells asked.

Gomez shook her head. "Just in the houses of people who normally celebrate Christmas. Obviously mostly Christians and people who share that cultural tradition, but it depends. Uh, one of my counterparts in the Japanese defense forces said that buckets of KFC chicken started to spontaneously appear around them."

Kells furrowed his brow at that. "What?"

"The Japanese eat KFC for Christmas," Tim said. Eyes turned to him. "I was at Kadena Air Force Base in Okinawa for a year. It's a thing. It started in the '70s."

Kells turned back to Gomez. "What else?"

"As far as we can tell, it's not just Christmas," Gomez said. "It's a really *nice* Christmas."

"What does that mean?"

"It means that the gifts are really nice and are what the recipients would actually want," Gomez said. "People are reporting high-end electronics and clothes and sporting equipment."

"I got the putter I've been lusting after for two years," Hibbens said.

"Who knew that you wanted it?" Kells asked.

Hibbens snorted. "Hell, *everybody* knew I wanted it. I've been dropping hints to Kathy and the kids since my birthday a year ago. It's not a secret."

"My kids got a PlayStation and a stack of games," Barker said. "I was planning to get the new generation of the console for my son as a birthday present next month. But I was beaten to the punch."

"Have any manufacturers reported thefts of inventory?" Dunwoody said, to Gomez.

"Ma'am?"

"Where are these putters and PlayStations and buckets of KFC coming from?" Dunwoody asked.

"We haven't heard from manufacturers or stores that there's inventory missing," Gomez said.

"So these presents are just materializing out of thin air."

"Yes, ma'am. Literally and figuratively." Dunwoody sat back in her chair, considering this.

"And how, exactly, are they doing that?" Kells asked.

Gomez looked over to Hibbens, who took the question. "We don't know, Mr. Secretary. We're looking into it. By all accounts it shouldn't be possible."

"Unless you're Santa Claus," Dunwoody said. This got a general laugh. Tim looked over to his boss and noticed she wasn't laughing.

Neither was Kells. "Are we done with the funny comments?" he asked. "This represents a huge security issue."

"It wasn't an attack," Hibbens pointed out.

"Wasn't it?" Kells countered. "Under any other circumstance, would you welcome an invasion of your home, Chuck? You got a nice putter out of it. Great. Who's to say the next time it's not going to be a bomb, or a biological agent, or something worse?"

Kells looked around the table. "I'm going to have to go back to the White House and tell the President that not only does our military not have any idea of how this happened, but that it also doesn't have a plan for keeping it from happening again—not *Christmas*, to be clear. The part where millions of American homes are invaded by an invisible force of immense capability, who because of that capability could destroy us as easily as it drops off presents."

He stood, and everyone stood with him. "It's eight a.m. now. I'll be back here at two for another briefing. Between now and then someone better find me some answers. Don't make me go back to the President empty-handed twice. You know how she is. Don't disappoint either of us." Kells left in a flurry of assistants.

"That went well," Barker muttered to Tim, and then went over to his boss. Tim nodded and looked over at his own boss. Dunwoody looked lost in thought, silent and still where everyone else was collecting their materials and talking.

Tim went over to her. "Everything all right, General?"

"I'm fine," she said, and looked Tim over. "You busy right now, Major?"

"I'm as busy as you need me to be, ma'am."

Dunwoody nodded. "I need you to make a trip for me, then."

AN HOUR and a half later Tim Collier pulled his government-issue, decade-old American-made gray sedan into the unpaved parking lot of the Palentine Christmas Tree Farm in Friendship, Maryland. An old man watched Tim drive up and park and emerge from the car.

"You are either very early or very late for a Christmas tree," the old man said to Tim.

"I'm not here for a Christmas tree," Tim said to him.

"Are you lost?" the old man asked. "We used to get lost souls here all the time, needing direction one way or another. Google Maps mostly took care of that, though. Nowadays the only people who come here intend to."

"That's me," Tim said.

"But you're not here for a Christmas tree."

"No, sir."

"Well, that's just as well, since I wouldn't sell one to you," the old man said. "Too early in the season."

"I already have one," Tim noted. "It arrived in my house this morning. I have no idea how it got there."

"Oh, yes. That happened today, didn't it?"

"Didn't you get a Christmas tree too?" Tim asked.

The old man smiled and motioned to the Christmas tree farm around them. "You think I would notice another one?"

Tim smiled at this. The old man smiled back. "So you're not here for a tree and you're not lost. What, young man, what are you here for?"

"Are you Leon Abernathy?"

"That's me."

"Then I have a message for you from General Mavis Dunwoody."

The old man who was Abernathy looked puzzled for a moment, and then his eyes brightened. "Mavis! It's been years. She's a general now?"

"She is."

"Well, good for her. It doesn't surprise me. She was always smart and ambitious. I'm happy to hear that she remembers me. Although," and here he motioned to Tim, "I'm not sure why she had you come all this way. Our email address is on our website. She could have just sent a note."

Tim, who had noted the "aol.com" email address on the web site that did not look like it had been updated since 1996, nodded at this. "She believed this particular message was best delivered in person."

"Did she now." Abernathy looked Tim over, and then motioned. "Well, then, come on. If we're going to do business too important for email, then we might as well have a cup of coffee to go with it." Abernathy started walking toward a low-slung building. Tim followed.

The building was a store, (which (and, Tim decided, rather unsurprisingly) featured) Christmas-themed trinkets, ornaments and decorations. Abernathy made his way through the store toward a back room. Tim followed but Abernathy waved him off and pointed to a small nook, where two red chairs with green trimming sat. "Go ahead and take a seat while I get the coffee. How do you take yours?"

"Black," Tim said.

Abernathy smiled at this. "Ah, fearless. Sit, sit. I'll be right back out."

Tim sat and looked around at the Christmas decorations and ornaments festooned about the shop. They were not the standard-issue decorations you could buy at Wal-Mart and Hallmark; everything appeared handmade and meticulously crafted. Abernathy noticed Tim looking at them as he came out with two mugs. "See anything you like?"

"I like them all," Tim said.

"Well, thank you." Abernathy handed Tim his mug and sat down.

"Did you make them?"

"What? No, no." Abernathy waved at the decorations. "I couldn't manage anything like these. They're made for me."

"By whom?"

"By elves, of course!" Abernathy chuckled at his own joke and nodded at Tim. "How's your coffee?"

Tim tried his drink. "It's good."

"Good. I don't do anything fancy with it, just good beans and hot water. I sell eggnog and Christmas mint flavored coffee over there by the cash register during the season, but I don't drink it myself. Seems like an expensive way to ruin coffee. Now." Abernathy set his mug down on the small side table by his chair. "What's Mavis' message?"

"She said she needed to see your boss."

"My boss."

"Yes, sir. She also said that it was urgent and that the sooner it could be arranged, the better, for everyone."

"Who is 'everyone' in this scenario, young man?"

"I'm not sure, but I think it probably includes the President."

"Her! Well." Abernathy seemed impressed by this. He picked up his mug and took a long sip, looking over the mug to Tim. "Did the general explain to you who my boss is?"

"No, sir."

"Who do you think my boss is?"

"I have no idea," Tim admitted.

"You don't ask questions," Abernathy prompted.

"I have many, many questions," Tim said. "But at the moment I'm keeping them to myself and doing what the general asked me to do, which is to deliver her message to you. I'm also supposed to tell her what your reply is."

"So you have no curiosity who my boss is."

Tim looked around. "This looks to me like a one-man or one-family operation. I wouldn't think you'd have a boss at all. So if you have a boss, it's probably not a formal one. Not one you'd get a W-2 form from."

Abernathy got a twinkle in his eye at this. "You think this tree farm is a front!"

"Maybe?" Tim ventured.

"Who for? The mafia? The Russians? Drug cartels? Big oil?"

"Maybe the Chinese," Tim said, acknowledging Abernathy's gently sardonic tone. "The Chinese have the manufacturing infrastructure to make millions of gifts, and perhaps the technology to deliver them in this way."

"The Chinese!" Abernathy literally slapped his knee, which was a thing that Tim had read about but couldn't remember anyone actually doing. "Well, I suppose that if you're trying to think rationally about this, they're a good choice."

"Did I get it right?" Tim asked.

"How was your Christmas, young man?" Abernathy asked.

"You mean this morning," Tim asked, by way of clarification.

"Yes."

"It was nice," Tim admitted. "My son and daughter got a ton of gifts. Gifts that were well chosen for them. They were delighted."

"And you? Any gifts for you?"

"Just one."

"That doesn't seem like that many."

"I don't usually ask for gifts at all."

"Why not?"

"I don't like people to feel like they have to get me anything," Tim said.

Abernathy nodded. "A very mature attitude. I expect people hate that about you."

"They do, actually."

"What was the gift?"

"A book," Tim said. And not just a book, a first edition of a book he loved as a teenager, one that spoke to him and had gotten him through some rough times. When Tim had opened the book, he saw that the title page had been signed by the author. Tim guessed that particular first edition was probably worth a couple thousand dollars on eBay.

"Good book?" Abernathy asked.

"For me, yes."

"Not something the Chinese would have mass produced, though," Abernathy prompted.

"Probably not," Tim agreed.

Abernathy nodded, took another sip from his mug, and stood up. Tim started to rise as well but Abernathy motioned him back into his seat. "I've got to go call Beijing," he said, again chuckling at his own joke. "See if my boss will meet yours." He motioned at the shop. "Why don't you have a look around. See if there's something that appeals to you. I won't be a minute." Abernathy headed to the back of the shop.

Tim got up and looked around the shop, taking special notice of the delicate and intricate tree ornaments. One in particular caught his eye, one representing a family: two adults, two children, all of them happy to be together. The ornament was stylized to the point of being almost abstract, but it affected Tim nevertheless. He imagined his own family in the same poses, joyous in each other's company. He reached out to touch it and was surprised to feel a small lump in his throat.

"You found one you like," Abernathy said, from behind him.

Tim jumped a tiny bit, startled by the sudden appearance of the old man.

"Sorry," Abernathy said.

Tim smiled. "It's all right."

Abernathy looked past Tim to the ornament. "That's a nice one."

"It reminded me of my own family."

"It's supposed to," Abernathy said, and then looked back to Tim. "I got in touch my boss. He said he's awfully busy at the moment but that he will send a representative to meet with Mavis today at one p.m."

"Where?"

"It doesn't matter where, our representative will find her."

Tim raised his eyebrows. "The Pentagon's not exactly an easy place to get into."

Abernathy smiled. "You'd be surprised. Also, my boss suggests that you invite Secretary Kells to the meeting. After all, is this meeting not for his information and benefit?"

"How do you know that?" Tim asked.

"I suppose you could also invite the President herself," Abernathy continued, without answering the question. "But I suspect she's busy today." Abernathy looked up at Tim, and then patted his shoulder. "Sorry, young man. I didn't mean to disconcert you."

Tim was disconcerted anyway. "I don't understand how you know these details," he said.

"Beijing knows a lot," Abernathy said, and then caught Tim's expression. "That was a joke. Your boss can explain this to you later, I suppose. In the meantime, you better get going. If Mavis didn't want to email the request to me, then she's probably not going to want a text or phone call from you. You should probably deliver the message in person. Which means you'll have to hurry if you want to get everyone in that conference room at one o'clock."

Abernathy walked past Tim, plucked the ornament from its display tree, and handed it to him. "Take this. A gift."

"I couldn't possibly," Tim began, but Abernathy held up a hand.

"I know, you don't want me to feel I have to. The good news is, I don't have to. I just want to. That's the thing about gifts, Major Collier. They're not obligations. They're a kindness. You're having a confusing day. I think you could use a little kindness right about now. So please, accept this gift."

"Thank you," Tim said, took the ornament and then walked to his car to drive back to the Pentagon. It wasn't until he was parking his car that he remembered that Abernathy had used his name while giving him the ornament, and that he hadn't given his name to Abernathy at any point in the conversation.

"I DON'T understand," Secretary Kells said to General Dunwoody. "You're saying NORAD knows what this is about, and didn't see fit to tell any of the rest of us."

General Dunwoody sighed in that way that Tim recognized meant she was trying to explain something difficult to someone unusually dense, and tried again. "No, sir. I'm not saying that NORAD had any special notice of what's happening now. They didn't. What I am saying is that my own experiences at NORAD two decades ago gave me some insight into what's going on today. Enough so that I asked Major Collier here," Dunwoody motioned to Tim, "to contact someone who I felt might be able to give us additional clarity about today's events."

"You know people who can just pop into and out of Americans' homes and leave gifts and Christmas hams," General Hibbens said.

"And you didn't tell any of us about this," Kells said.

"It's been classified for years," Dunwoody replied.

"I'm your boss," Kells snapped. "I have clearance."

"It's not that simple," Dunwoody said.

"It actually is that simple," Kells retorted. "And unless you start explaining what's going on, you're going to be finding yourself out of a job."

"Explanations are coming," Dunwoody said.

"That's great," Kells said. "When?"

The door to the conference room opened and a very short woman walked in. She picked a chair opposite at the table from Kells and sat in it.

Kells stared at the very short woman for a moment. "Who are you?" he asked.

"I'm Flora Jones," she said.

"And you are here because?"

"I'm here because my boss sent me to explain things to you, so you can explain things to your boss."

"And who is your boss?" Hibbens asked.

Jones smiled. "I'll tell you but you're not going to believe me."

"Try us," Kells said.

"Santa sent me," Jones said.

Tim estimated the silence lasted a good five seconds. Then Kells stood up. "This is waste of my time," he said.

"A leaded crystal decanter," Jones said.

Kells paused. "Excuse me?"

"Your gift this morning," Jones replied. "It was a leaded crystal decanter, was it not? You've wanted one for a while now, but your wife always talked you out of one. Said she didn't want to serve drinks in anything with lead in it. Even when you pointed out that it was fine unless the spirits were stored for a long period of time in one, she was not convinced. So you never got one. And this morning, there was one under the tree for you. Correct?"

"That's right, but," Kells began.

Jones ignored him and pointed to Dunwoody. "You got a complete Blu-Ray collection of *Friends*, which you've been meaning to get for years." She pointed at Tim. "You have a signed first edition." She pointed at Colonel Margie Gomez. "You received your grandmother's loose-leaf cookbook, which you thought was lost." She pointed to Hibbens. "And you got that putter, but of course you already told everyone about that. Did I list everyone's gifts correctly?"

Everyone nodded. "Good. Now look under your seats, please."

There was a moment of awkward shuffling and reaching under seats, and then everyone came up with something. Kells came up with a bottle of Redbreast 15-year-old Irish Whiskey. Dunwoody had a signed Hootie and the Blowfish CD. Gomez found a faded family photo. Hibbens had a six-pack of Titleist golf balls. Tim found a beautiful iridescent bookmark.

Kells stared at his whiskey and then back at Jones. "I don't understand."

"You understand just fine," Jones said. "You just don't want to believe." Jones pointed at Dunwoody again. "She didn't want to believe either, years ago, when she found out that NORAD really was tracking something in the skies on Christmas Eve."

"Santa's sleigh?" Hibbens asked, incredulously.

"Sure, let's call it that," Jones said. "Just like you call my boss Santa and you could call me an elf. Quibbling over specific words is missing the point."

"But you don't actually do things like this," Tim said, holding up his bookmark. "Fly around the world giving gifts, I mean. *We* do that. 'Santa' for my kids is me and my wife."

"We do what we're asked to do," Jones replied. "This year we were asked to deliver Christmas in July. You couldn't do it—you all expect Christmas in December, so it wouldn't have occurred to you that this year Christmas might move up in the schedule. So we had to pick up the slack."

"But Christmas is in December," Kells said. "It's Jesus' birthday."

Jones pivoted her head toward Kells. "Secretary Kells, this is really *not* the time to get into a long discussion about how early Christians positioned Christmas to take advantage of the winter solstice festivals that were already occurring, or how Christmas falls on a different day depending on which church you belong to, or even how Christmas' actual position in the seasons drifted before the Gregorian calendar. Christmas celebrates the birth of Christ, but it's not *actually* Jesus' birthday. That being the case, Christmas can fall whenever it needs to. This year, that was July 18th."

"Okay, but why?" Dunwoody asked. "Why July this year?"

"Because that's what we were asked to do."

"By whom?" Hibbens inquired.

"You'll remember when I said that quibbling over specific words is missing the point," Jones said. "So let's just agree that my boss has his own boss and not worry over the details."

"But why did…your boss's boss change the date?" Kells asked, irritably.

"Do you always tell your underlings why you do things?" Jones asked back to Kells. "We were told to do it. We did it. And we did a pretty good job of it, I have to say."

"What about December?" Tim asked.

"What about it?" Jones replied.

"You were told we'd be having Christmas in July this year," Tim said. "What's happening in December?"

Jones smiled what Tim would not have described as a perfectly warm smile. "Finally, someone is asking the right question."

"So what *is* happening in December?" Kells asked.

"Nothing," Jones said.

"What does that mean?" Kells persisted.

"It means exactly that." Jones looked around the table. "We have nothing scheduled for December. Not one thing."

"Why not?" Dunwoody asked.

"I don't know," Jones admitted. "I wasn't told, and neither was my boss."

"But you know enough to put two and two together," Kells said. "You were told to have Christmas in July. There is nothing on your schedule for December. You have to have an *opinion* on why that is."

"You don't want to know what *my* opinion is," Jones said.

"What about your boss's opinion?" Tim asked.

Jones smiled again. "Do you know why you get gifts on Christmas?" she asked the room.

"Everyone likes gifts," Kells said.

"Not true, and also missing the point," Jones said, and then turned to Tim. "You know why."

"They're a kindness," Tim said.

"Yes." Jones looked around the room. "When you give a gift, you are presenting kindness. You are showing the person that you see them. That you appreciate them. That you want something for them that will ease their burdens and the load they carry. You want to make them happy, if only for a moment. A gift is a kindness."

"So we need kindness now?" Dunwoody asked.

"You tell me," Jones said. "Humans are not really very kind to each other, are they? It's never been your strong suit, but especially these days you seem to be terrible to each other. You're not very kind to your planet recently, either, are you? You're running a surplus of plastic and carbon dioxide, for sure. Kindness? Not so much. Maybe this is a reminder from above that a little kindness goes a long way."

"Or that we'll need kindness for what's to come," Tim said. "Something to ease our burdens and lighten our load. To make us happy, if only for a moment."

Jones nodded. "Or that, perhaps. December is unscheduled, after all."

"What does that mean?" Kells asked, after a moment.

Jones spread her hands, helplessly. "I don't know. I can't tell you what the future is. But I can tell you what my boss has said to me. He tells me that our future will be what we make of it today. And today, you've received kindness. You've gotten it early this year. What you do with it is up to you. Today, tomorrow, all the way to December and, possibly, beyond that. That's what I've come here to tell you. And now that I have, I'm going."

Kells blinked. "That's it?"

"That's enough," Jones said, turning her attention back to Tim. "If you know what to do with it."

"I still want to know how your boss got into our houses."

"Don't worry, Secretary Kells," Jones said. "Santa's not going to license the tech to the commies or the terrorists. Tell your president and anyone else who's worried that they're safe." She pushed her seat back and jumped down. She looked over to Dunwoody. "The boss says hello." Dunwoody smiled at that. Jones headed to door.

"Ms. Jones," Tim said, as she reached the doorknob.

Jones looked back.

"Merry Christmas."

Jones smiled and left.

TIM CAME home to a house filled with the sound of Christmas carols and the smells of ham and pumpkin pie.

"It feels ridiculous to be making Christmas dinner," Evie said, to Tim. "It's eighty-five degrees outside. But then I remembered that in the southern hemisphere they have Christmas in the summer."

"We're having an Australian Christmas!" Kerry said.

"Stralman!" Damie echoed.

"It makes as much sense as anything else today," Evie concluded.

"That works for me." Tim reached into his jacket pocket and pulled out the ornament he'd been given by Abernathy. He showed it to Kerry and Damie. "Take a look at this," he said.

Kerry looked at it. "It's our family," she said, after a second.

"I think it is," Tim agreed. He handed it to her. "Why don't you go put it on the tree." Kerry grinned widely and scampered over to the tree, Damie following.

"So, how did it happen?" Evie asked. She motioned to encompass the house. "This. Everything."

"Santa," Tim said.

"I'm serious."

"I'm pretty sure I am too."

Evie looked at her husband and decided not to press it. "I invited Cinda Lundburgh to dinner," she said. "You know she's by herself since Bill died."

"I remember."

"Yeah. So," Evie shrugged. "I thought it would be nice to ask her to come. It's Christmas. Sort of."

Tim gave his wife a hug and a kiss. "It's definitely Christmas. And you were kind to invite her."

"Well, you know," Evie said. "That's what Christmas is for."

Tim smiled at that, and then went to go look at the tree, because Kerry very much wanted to show him where she put the ornament, and Damie very much wanted him to look, too.

INTERVIEW WITH SANTA'S REINDEER WRANGLER

Q: Your name and occupation, please.

A: I'm Naseem Copely, and I'm the Reindeer Corps Manager for Santa Claus.

Q: What does that title mean?

A: Basically I'm responsible for recruiting, outfitting and caring for the reindeer who pull Santa's sleigh on Christmas. If it has anything to do with the reindeer, I'm the one in charge of it.

Q: Why would you need to recruit? We already know who the reindeer are. Dasher and Dancer and Prancer and so on.

A: Well, that's the first misconception. The canonical names of the reindeer aren't of the reindeer themselves. The canonical names describe the *role* of the reindeer.

Q: I'm not sure I follow.

A: So, it's like this: You have a football team, right? And a football team has a quarterback and fullbacks and half-backs and centers and such. And in the role of quarterback, you could have Eli Manning or Andrew Luck or Aaron Rodgers or whomever.

Q: Okay.

A: So on a reindeer team, there's a Dasher and a Dancer and a Prancer and so on. They're roles. They're positions. And the *position* of Dasher, as an example, is currently held by a reindeer named Buckletoe McGee. And before her, it was held by Tinselhart Flaherty, and before her, Ted Cruz.

Q: Ted Cruz.

A: Yes. No relation.

Q: All right. So the canonical names are the role of the reindeer, but this leaves open the question of why there are roles at all.

A: Because of the weather and various atmospheric conditions, basically. Depending on the weather, one or another of the team will be in lead position.

Q: So, for example—

A: So if the weather is clear, then Dasher is in the lead, because she's fast and good with straight lines. If there's a lot of turbulence in the upper atmosphere, then Dancer's in front, because she's good finding pockets of calm air for Santa to navigate into. "Donner" is the German word for "thunder," so our Donner's up when we have thunderstorms, and so on.

Q: Okay, but what about Cupid?

A: In the lead when we have to sweet-talk our way out of a moving violation citation.

Q: That really happens?

A: Lots of little towns have speed traps, man. They don't care if it's Santa. You see Santa, they see a wealthy traveler who won't come back to town to contest a ticket.

Q: How does that even work? A reindeer mitigating traffic violations, I mean.

A: It's technical. Very technical. I'd need graphs and a chart.

Q: And Vixen? What role does Vixen play?

A: Uh, that role's currently in transition.

Q: What does that mean?

A: It means I'm ready for your next question.

Q: All right, what about the Rudolph position?

A: (Sighs) There is *no* Rudolph position. Never *was*. Never *will* be.

Q: You seem annoyed by this question.

A: None of us up here at the pole are big fans of the whole "Rudolph" thing.

Q: Why not?

A: Well, it makes us look like jerks, doesn't it? A young reindeer is discriminated against up to and until he has marginal utility. I mean, really. Who looks good in that scenario? Not all of the other reindeer, who come across as bigots and bullies. And not *Santa*, who is implicitly tacit in reindeer bigotry.

Q: I have to admit I never really thought about it that hard.

A: You know, here at the pole we work hard to make sure that everyone feels welcome—it's not just a legal requirement, it's the whole ethos behind the Santa organization. And this one song craps on that for a reindeer who *never even existed?* Yeah, we're not happy.

Q: You could sue for defamation.

A: No one comes out ahead when you do that. Anyway, Santa has his way of dealing with things like this.

Q: What do you mean?

A: Let's just say a certain songwriter received lots of coal one year. In his car. The one with the white bucket seats.

Q: Okay. The next question: Why reindeer?

A: Why not reindeer?

Q: Generally speaking, they don't actually fly.

A: Neither do sleighs, generally speaking, and yet here we are.

Q: We could talk about that. I mean, the general violation of physics that goes on around the whole Santa's sleigh thing.

A: Look, I don't pretend to know the science of the flying sleigh thing, okay? That's not my job. You can ask Santa's physicists about it if you want.

Q: Santa has physicists on staff?

A: Of course he does. He's one of the largest recruiters of physicists outside of NASA. What, you thought all this happened because of magic?

Q: Well, now that you mention it, yes. Yes, I did.

A: See, that's just silly. It's not magic. It's technology. Highly, highly advanced technology.

Q: So technology makes the reindeer fly.

A: No, that's genetic.

Q: Oh, come *on*.

A: You'll have to interview some of Santa's biologists about that.

Q: Leaving aside the questionable physics and biology of flying reindeer, how do you recruit them? The reindeer, that is.

A: Craigslist.

Q: You're telling me the reindeer can read.

A: Of course not. That's just ridiculous.

Q: Unlike them *flying*.

A: It's not the reindeer, it's their owners. Laplanders and Canadians have access to the internet too.

Q: So the owners of the reindeer show up with their deer, and then what?

A: Well, the genes for flying in reindeer are recessive, so we have to test for ability.

Q: With a DNA test?

A: With a catapult.

Q: Wait, what?

A: We chuck 'em into the air and see what happens.

Q: That's…that's *horrible*.

A: Why?

Q: What if they don't have the flying gene!

A: Then they come down.

Q: And you don't see a problem with that?

A: It's just gravity.

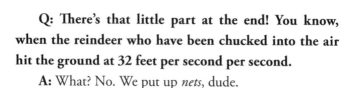
Q: There's that little part at the end! You know, when the reindeer who have been chucked into the air hit the ground at 32 feet per second per second.

A: What? No. We put up *nets*, dude.

Q: Nets?

A: Nets. To catch them. Jeez, what do you think we are, monsters?

Q: I didn't know!

A: PETA would be *all over us* for that.

Q: Maybe you should have mentioned the nets earlier.

A: I would think they would be *implied*.

Q: Sorry.

A: *Anyway.*

Q: Okay, so you sorted the ones who can fly from the ones who can't. What then?

A: Then we take the new reindeer and start training them, using various tests and exercises to see which role they would be best at.

Q: The fabled Reindeer Games.

A: Right. Once we know who is good at what, we slot them into the role.

Q: So how many reindeer are in each position?

A: Roughly a hundred.

Q: That's...a lot of reindeer.

A: What did you expect?

Q: I don't know, I thought maybe two or three for each position. Like a football team.

A: That was just an *analogy*.

Q: No, right, I get that, but even so.

A: Look, these are animals. They get tired. And the sleigh crosses the entire planet. You can't have a single team of eight physical animals pull a heavy object that entire distance. That's cruel. You got a swap 'em out at regular intervals. So the couple of days before Christmas we truck them to various places around the world, and when Santa lands, we make the swap.

Q: Where do these swapouts usually happen?

A: Typically mall parking lots. They swap out and Santa can take a bathroom break. He's drinking lots of milk that night and eating a metric ton of cookies. He's gotta make space.

Q: And no one notices Santa landing and swapping out the team.

A: We're quick about it.

Q: How quick?

A: Let me put it this way: NASCAR pit crews?

Q: Yes?

A: Slackers.

Q: Final question: the reindeer are on the job one night of the year.

A: Correct.

Q: What are they doing the rest of the year?

A: Leipäjuusto.

Q: Gesundheit.

A: I didn't sneeze, you numbskull. It's a traditional Scandinavian cheese originally made from reindeer milk.

Q: Santa's a cheesemaker on the side, is what you're saying.

A: And a damn fine one. His Leipäjuusto did very well at the International Cheese Awards this year.

Q: Did he say "Merry Curdmas" when he won?

A: No.

Q: Maybe he could make Holy Infant Cheddar, whose selling points would be that it's tender and mild.

A: Stop.

Q: "Ho Ho Havarti!"

A: I'm going to have Vixen stab you with an antler now.

8 THINGS YOU DIDN'T KNOW YOU DIDN'T KNOW ABOUT YOUR FAVORITE HOLIDAY MUSIC

Each year we hear them, we sing them, we love them: The holiday songs of our lives. But how much do we really know about the great music of the holidays? Probably not as much as we think. And thus, to celebrate the holiday season, I am delighted to present to you **8 Things You Didn't Know You Didn't Know About Your Favorite Holiday Music.** I assure you each of these nuggets of knowledge is just as true as the one before it.

"Let it Snow"

WHILE IT is well known that the song was written in 1945 by Jule Styne and Sammy Cahn in July, in southern California, on one of the hottest days of that year, what is not commonly known is that Styne and Cahn both penned the song while sitting in a large tub filled to the brim with ice cubes. "We just couldn't get it right and we realized that on that day, in that place, we were just too far from inspiration," lyricist Cahn would write in his 1975 autobiography, *I Should Care.* "A couple hundred pounds of ice fixed that right up."

While the inspiration worked, yielding a number one tune and an enduring holiday classic, composer Styne unfortunately suffered a severe case of frostbite and narrowly missed having to amputate three toes on his left foot. He vowed never to work that way again. Cahn, however, used this "immersive songwriting" technique for several other songs, most memorably writing "Three Coins in the Fountain" in an inflatable pool while an assistant trained a garden hose at his head.

"Baby, It's Cold Outside"

FRANK LOESSER penned this classic in 1944 and performed it as a duet with his wife at a party, signifying to guests that it was getting close to the time they should depart. However Loesser, whose successes with *Guys and Dolls* and *How to Succeed in Business Without Really Trying* were still years in the future, repurposed the song for an aborted 1946 musical called *That Damned Winter,* in which the fictional town of Penobscroggin, Maine was confronted with the worst blizzard in 150 years, leading the formerly placid citizens of the picturesque New England hamlet to engage in violence, murder and ritual cannibalism.

In the play, the song was performed in a plaintive, minor key, with the lead begging his love not to leave, lest she freeze to death in the howling wind outside or alternately be absconded with by the nefarious Tucker family next door, the only Penobscroggin family not to appear to suffer from the icy famine, although several of their neighbors had gone missing. She leaves anyway and disappears, with only a shoe to mark her passing, but in the emotional finale returns alive in the spring, having been sheltered during the winter by adorable woodland animals, which then viciously and hungrily attack the corpulent, slow-moving Tuckers.

Despite an impressive book by playwright Thornton Wilder, *That Damned Winter* lasted only one performance in an out-of-town tryout in Sacramento, at which several descendants of the Donner Party began a riot during intermission. After the debacle, Loesser, disheartened, burned the score to the play, saving only "Baby," the rights to which he sold to film studio MGM.

"Rudolph the Red-Nosed Reindeer"

THE STORY of Rudolph is most famously known as a song, memorably performed by Gene Autry in 1949. However, the song is an adaptation of a 1939 poem by Robert L. May, initially written at the behest of the Montgomery Ward department store, which originally published the poem in a coloring book, distributing 2.4 million copies during the holidays. Despite the light tone of the poem, "Rudolph" is known to be a vicious satire of one Rudy Padgett, a contemporary of May's with whom the writer shared a bitter, lifelong rivalry. The reindeer's famous red nose is actually a metaphor for Padgett's alcoholism, with the other "reindeer" (Padgett and May's companions) laughing, calling him names and refusing to play with him not because of bigotry but because they were mocking his lack of control around booze.

The original ending of "Rudolph" had a soft-hearted Santa letting Rudolph take part in the sleigh team over the objections of the other reindeer, leading to the sleigh being wrapped around a tree, six of the eight traditional reindeer killed and Christmas cancelled, much to the dismay of children everywhere. The executives at Montgomery Ward, however, said that this version was "too dark for a coloring book" and ordered a rewrite, which May grudgingly provided. Ironically and coincidentally, after the publication of "Rudolph," Rudy Padgett sobered up and became a beloved member of his community, which only seemed to enrage May all the more. "My father would often ask Uncle Bob what the deal was between him and Rudy," economist Steven Levitt, May's grand-nephew, once wrote in *Slate*. "Uncle Bob would only mutter one word, darkly: 'Pencils.' We never learned what it meant. It's become our family's 'Rosebud.'"

"White Christmas"

THIS IMMORTAL Irving Berlin tune first became a hit for singer Bing Crosby in 1942 and then in many subsequent years afterward—which became a problem for Crosby, who had initially doubted the potential popularity of the song and said so to songwriter Irving Berlin. Berlin responded by making Crosby solemnly promise at the end of each year to take a shot of whiskey, one after another, for each week the song was on the charts. This required Crosby to down 11 sequential shots of whiskey in early 1943, with subsequent and dangerous whiskey sessions after the '45 and '46 holiday seasons, during which time the song returned to #1 on the charts. The song would go on to sell more than 50 million copies.

Realizing the dimensions of the true, cirrhotic danger in which he had placed both Crosby and his liver, Berlin released the crooner from his vow, allowing him to substitute whiskey shots with tokes from a marijuana cigarette instead. This pleased Crosby, who in the '60s and '70s would advocate for marijuana legalization.

"Little Drummer Boy"

THIS 1941 tune by Katherine Kennicott Davis has charmed generations with its tale of a young drummer playing his instrument to the delight of the newborn messiah. But this simple tune had a difficult birth, as Davis changed the profession of the little protagonist a number of times before settling on the role of drummer. Davis' archives at Wellesley College feature early drafts entitled "Little Trumpet Boy," "Little Ocarina Boy," "Little Didgeridoo Boy," "Little Mime Boy," "Little Short Order Cook Boy," "Little Public Relations Intern Boy," "Little Gastroenterologist Boy" and "Little Kid Who Just Wandered By and Was Confusingly Pushed Into a Barn Boy."

Most of these drafts were only fragments, although Davis completed "Little Didgeridoo Boy" and had it performed for Australian Prime Minister Robert Menzies during a 1964 trip to the United States. Menzies was reported to ask Davis how a didgeridoo happened to be anywhere near Bethlehem in biblical times. Davis would later write disparagingly of Menzies' "Philistine musical nature" and shoved that version of the song into a box. In 2001, musical artist Madonna was reported to have considered recording the didgeridoo version with herself playing the instrument, but the idea was shelved to avoid offending Australian aboriginal sensibilities. Madonna went on to make the film *Swept Away* instead.

"Feliz Navidad"

DURING THE 1990 invasion of Panama by the United States, US military forces surrounded the Vatican embassy, where dictator Manuel Noriega had fled, and engaged in psychological warfare with the fugitive leader by blasting rock music, which he loathed. But it wasn't until US played "Feliz Navidad" on a repeating loop that Noriega finally surrendered on January 3, 1991. In 2004, journalist Guillermo Hernandez, who was part of the US forces who captured Noriega, wrote in *Rolling Stone,* "His first words as he left the embassy were 'That f**king song. That *f**king song.* Why couldn't you just keep playing Led Zeppelin?'"

Prior to Noriega's 1992 trial, the former dictator's lawyers attempted to derail the trial by filing a motion suggesting that repeated playing of "Feliz Navidad" constituted a violation of the Geneva Conventions. The judge, while stating his sympathy for the argument, denied the petition.

"Wonderful Christmastime"

IN A 1994 interview with *Q* magazine on the occasion of the 15th anniversary of the release of the Wings album *Back to the Egg*, producer Chris Thomas recalled that, after consuming a particularly large vegetarian burrito, Paul McCartney had bet Thomas one thousand pounds that he could write a hit song in the same amount of time it took him to unload his bowels. "I said, 'you're on,' and he went to the loo," said Thomas. "Five minutes later he came out, went over to the Prophet-5 I had in the studio, and there was 'Wonderful Christmastime.' When it hit number six on the British charts, he sent me a note that said 'Right then, a thousand quid.' I sent him an invoice for damages to the studio loo caused by his vegetarian burrito, which came to a thousand quid." Thomas would later recant the interview, under mysterious circumstances.

In 1999, in an *NME* poll entitled "Explain 'Wonderful Christmastime,'" 46% of that magazine's respondents chose the poll option that said that the existence of the song proved there was no God, but that there might be a devil. Another 39% chose the response that said that yes, the song sucked, but at least it didn't have Yoko on it, a clear reference to fellow Beatle John Lennon's "Happy Xmas (the War is Over)."

Rumors that George Michael wrote the hit holiday tune "Last Christmas" under similar circumstances are to date unsubstantiated.

"Silent Night"

IN THE late 1800s, this classic carol, first composed in 1816 by German priest Joseph Mohr, almost fell out of the Christmas canon when an anti-Austrian remnant of the Huguenot church suggested that the lyrics of the carol were not about adoring the Virgin Mary and the infant Jesus, but consuming them hungrily—thus the descriptions of both mother and child as "round" (i.e., deliciously plump) and infant Jesus himself as "tender and mild," like a good veal. This culminated in 1871 with the scholarly debate at the University of Heidelberg in which it was suggested that any hint of messiah consumption could be explained away as an allegorical reference to transubstantiation. This led to outraged Catholic students burning down the lecture hall.

Eventually the controversy waned, but to this day *kinderwurst*, a tender, mild veal sausage served *en flambe*, is a popular seasonal dish in southern Germany.

JACKIE JONES AND
MELROSE MANDY

Jackie Jones loved Christmas. She loved it a lot.
For the love and the sharing? As if! (or, perhaps, Not!).
Jackie loved Christmas more than most girls and boys
For one simple reason: Because of the toys!
Yes! Toys! By the bundle! By the truck! By the ton!
A big pile of toys is what made Christmas fun.

Was Jackie Jones spoiled? Well, maybe so;
She rarely said "please," and got angry at "no."
But was it her fault that she got what she wanted?
Was it her problem that she rarely was haunted
By the idea there just might be something more
Than mountains of presents laid out on the floor?

Whatever the cause for her toy-fueled obsession
This particular year Jackie had a confession:
The toy that she wanted very mostest of all
Was the Melrose Mandy high fashion doll.
It's not that she didn't want other toys—far from it!
But on her Christmas list, Mandy was high on the
     summit.

"But why?" Jackie Jones was asked one winter day
By a classmate of hers named Sophie McCray.
"You have dozens and dozens and dozens of dollies
"From Miami Marta to Hollywood Holly
"With their cars and their clothes! And so I ask you
"What more with Mandy would you possibly do?"

What would Jackie do? What *wouldn't* she do!
Jackie might not know much, but this much she knew
From the moment she saw Mandy on her TV screen
She knew that the doll was the key to her dreams.
With all the accessories and add-ons unfurled
With her doll Mandy, she could take on the world!

Jackie Jones could just see it now:
All the things she would do with her posable pal.
They would cruise Highway One, with the top down
In Mandy's convertible (in surf blue or sand brown)
Then get in Mandy's plane—the one with the pool
Not the one with the sauna (the sauna's not cool).

Mandy and she would fly all over the globe
Spreading joy and love through Mandy's hip line
   of clothes
And when the world's people had been accessorized
Jackie and Mandy would win the Peace Prize
And in matching peach shoes would cause a sensation
When they came to address the United Nations.

But how to explain this to Sophie McCray?
Sophie was poor and she lived far away
On the outskirts of town in a small little room
With just barely enough space for a doll or two.
Sophie was her friend, but she had to admit it
There was just no way Sophie would ever quite get it.

But now Christmas was coming, there was no time
   to lose!
Jackie let Mom and Dad know which gift to choose
She begged, she pleaded, she dropped a few hints
And then just to be sure, she threw a few fits.
Jackie made clear—so there was *no* doubt
Without her dear Mandy she'd do nothing but pout.

And then Christmas came! Jackie ran down the stairs
And begun tearing open the presents down there.
There were dozens of presents marked with her name
And Jackie dove into them all with no shame.
She attacked them with ferocity, ardor and glee
And came very close to toppling the tree.

And boy, what a haul: You could hardly conceive
Of the sheer loads of stuff hidden under that tree.
There was a bike and bird and some blocks and a box
That held a whole outfit that matched with her socks.
There were sparkly hair spangles, a karaoke machine
And a talking mechanical cat named Maureen.

There was a stuffed unicorn and video games
And a soft teddy bear that could remember your name.
There were card games, board games and puzzles
    and balls
And six gift certificates to six different malls.
We could go on, but it's obvious to all
That Jackie Jones had herself quite a haul.

But no Melrose Mandy! Mandy couldn't be found!
And you can be sure Jackie Jones looked around.
And when Jackie was certain the doll was unseen,
She drew in her breath for a lung-busting scream.
But that scream never happened; at the last second
Jackie's mom had a gift—and to her daughter she
    beckoned.

And then there she was in all of her glory!
Melrose Mandy and her whole inventory
Of accessories and costumes, of clothes and of shoes
More things that come separately than one girl
    could use.
Jackie let out a squeal, and grabbed Mandy tight
And said "I'm going to play with her all day and
    all night!"

And she did! Well, she *tried*. But sometime 'round noon
Jackie's obsession with Mandy just faltered and
   swooned.
It's not that Jackie didn't have fun—not at all.
But it turns out that Mandy *was* just another doll.
Like Miami Marta or Hollywood Holly,
Or any old Cindy, Mindy, Stacy or Molly.

Jackie went to her closet and turned on the light
And saw dozens of dolls there—it was quite a sight.
Dolls stretched back for yards, to the very first one
A cuddly plush doll named Bitsy Bygumm
A doll which Jackie—she did suddenly remember
Had promised her mom she would play with forever.

And suddenly Jackie had an interesting thought
About all the dolls she demanded be bought.
Each time, with each one, Jackie was sure
That this doll would be the one that would cure
All the things in her life with which she was bored
But it didn't—it couldn't—and Jackie wanted one more.

The dolls always changed, but I stayed the same
Jackie thought, and just then a light went on in her brain
No matter how many toys or dolls that she had
They themselves couldn't make her happy or sad.
What mattered was *her*—what mattered was whether
She chained all her happiness to toys like a tether.

And then Jackie thought of Sophie McCray
Sharing Christmas with family in her house far away.
She thought of her friend and remembered anew
"What more with Mandy would you possibly do?"
Then Jackie went down to talk to her mother
And made a request quite unlike any other.

Years later, Sophie would remember quite clearly
She almost missed that box! It was quite nearly
Covered in snow—it must have been out all night
But on the day after Christmas it was a delight
To open the box and see that inside
Was a gift that a stranger saw fit to provide.

And as for Jackie, well, she still liked her toys.
And still loved Christmas, like most girls and boys.
But toys she now knew were only for fun
And not things upon which one's dreams should be spun.
She loved Christmas now, because she'd come to believe
That it truly was better to give than receive.

What Jackie Jones knows, you can know too
Look in your soul and you'll see that it's true.
And come Christmas day, hug those you love dear
And remember today, and each year after year,
That getting is nice, but giving is better
Toys come and go, but love lasts forever.

AN INTERVIEW WITH THE CHRISTMAS BUNNY

Your name, please.

Aloysius McFuzz.

And your profession?

I am the Christmas Bunny.

The Christmas Bunny.

That is correct.

Not the Easter Bunny.

No, but close. But the Christmas Bunny is a franchise.

Franchise?

Yes. You know what a franchise is?

In the sense of McDonald's or Burger King franchising a store.

Yes.

Sure.

Same thing. Just with rabbits. And holidays.

I'm afraid I'm still not entirely clear on the concept here.

Fine. You said you know about the Easter Bunny.

I do.

The Easter Bunny is a very successful icon of his season and does a huge amount of business through licensing. Every Easter Bunny stuffed animal, toy, decoration, chocolate treat, what have you, he gets a cut. And through that initial influx of licensing deal cash, he moved into other sectors of Easter menagerie licensing. In 1985, for example, he bought out the entire Easter-related poultry segment. So everything Easter-related that features a bird or a bird product, he gets a cut of that too.

Including Easter eggs.

Oh, yeah. A gold mine, those. Even those chocolate creme eggs, you know which ones I'm talking about?

The ones that have the commercials where the rabbit clucks like a chicken.

That's how he got them! First, he sued them for trademark infringement on the rabbit. Then he got them on trademark infringement on the eggs. By the time the dust settled he had a substantial minority interest in the entire company.

Sounds ruthless.

He's no dumb bunny. But he does it all for the kids.

I still don't see how this has anything to do with Christmas, however.

Well, clearly, as the Easter Bunny shows, rabbits and holidays are a potent commercial mix, and in the course of time it became obvious that brand expansion needed to happen. But the Easter Bunny didn't want to do it himself—he didn't want to spread himself too thin—so he franchised it out and took bids on bunnies for the various holidays. I and my investors put in the strongest bid for Christmas.

I imagine there was a fair amount of competition for that particular holiday.

It was a challenging bidding environment, yes. It came down to us and Disney.

Disney.

Yes. They had re-acquired Oswald the Rabbit—that was Walt Disney's first famous animated character, and Universal had owned him until recently—and wanted to relaunch him.

I'm surprised they didn't get their way. Because, you know. It's Disney.

The Easter Bunny felt that since Christmas already has so many legacy characters, the Christmas Bunny should be new and fresh. I mean, Oswald's heyday was in the '20s. It's him and Felix the Cat, drinking prune juice in the retirement home.

How much were the franchise fees?

That's confidential.

Come on. You can tell me.

Let's just say it was more cheddar than the mouse wanted to shell out.

And there are other holiday bunnies, too.

Yes. At the franchise bidding, he sold the Thanksgiving Bunny, the July Fourth Bunny and the Labor Day Bunny.

There was interest in a Hanukkah Bunny and Kwanzaa Bunny too, but those are part of our franchise, so we'll eventually sub-franchise those.

No Valentine's Day Bunny.

No, he kept a two-month exclusivity window on either side of Easter. The National Arbor Day Foundation begged for an Arbor Day Bunny, and he totally shut them down. Had a tirade. The words "April is MINE" were said. It was an uncomfortable moment for everyone. But he had a point. You don't undercut your core brand. Especially not for Arbor Day.

Let's get back to Christmas again.

Yes, let's.

You noted that there are already several prominent...what did you call them?

"Legacy characters."

Several prominent legacy characters involved in the Christmas holiday. It seems like it may already be a saturated market in that respect.

This is true. But most of them are fairly minor and can either be eclipsed in popularity or simply bought out. To that end we are in serious negotiations with the Geisel estate. You probably know him as Dr. Seuss.

You're buying out the Grinch? That's oddly appropriate.

We're also pursuing a long-term license to Rudolph. We're already planning the stop-motion holiday special with me and him, saving the Island of Misfit Toys from Evil Drunken Santa.

Evil Drunken Santa.

Yes, that's right.

Isn't that defamation?

He's a public figure. We're on safe legal ground, First Amendment-wise.

You've settled on a plan of driving down Santa's popularity, then.

Well, yes, but that's actually only a minor component there. I was mentioning how we're dealing with the minor legacy characters. Well, there are two major ones.

Okay.

One's Jesus, and, well. He can't be touched.

Because he will smite you?

No, he's not the smiting type. But the Easter Bunny is. He says that he's got a good thing going with Easter, which is another Jesus-focused holiday, as you may be aware.

I'd heard.

Right. I was told in no uncertain terms that if I did anything against Jesus, the repercussions would be significant. The word "fricassee" was used, and not metaphorically.

I'm not sure I like what I'm learning about the Easter Bunny.

He is tough but fair.

So one is Jesus. I'm guessing the other is Santa Claus.

Yes. And him, I can totally go after. In fact, I was specifically told by the Easter Bunny to gun for him. Apparently there's bad blood there. I don't know the details. I don't want to know the details.

So what is your strategy for Santa?

We've developed a two-pronged approach. First, we're going to outcompete on service.

How so?

Think about it. Santa delivers on only one night, on an inflexible schedule, only to particular children, and in a manner that utterly compromises your home security—and he expects you to be happy about the arrangement.

I never thought about it that way.

No one does. Because it's the way it's always been done. But I ask you. Any other night, how would you react to a home invasion? At four a.m.? From a guy who judges your children? Which is of course an inherent criticism of you as a parent.

When you put it that way, Santa seems like a jerk.

And for all that, he expects cookies!

And milk!

The Christmas Bunny offers a better way. A two-week delivery window, on your schedule. We knock before we enter. And hey, we know that kids today have their ups and downs. We don't judge, either them or you. It's a no-pressure way to enjoy the holiday.

That's one prong. What's the other?

Litigation.

Litigation.

Yes.

As in, suing Santa Claus.

Absolutely.

For home invasion?

No, we don't have standing for that. But for restraint of trade, yes.

How does he restrain trade?

Are you kidding? The man's got the entire holiday locked up. We're trying to make deals with manufacturers and merchandisers here and abroad, and we're getting shown the door. They're not even allowing us to buy their stuff retail. We have to sneak into Target and Costco and try to buy things before they find us and kick us out.

I imagine your fluffy cotton tails give you away.

It's definitely not legal, what he's doing. So, yes, we'll be seeing Santa in court.

In US court? If anyone has jurisdiction over the North Pole, I would think it would be Canada or Russia.

Hey, the North Shore of Alaska is up there. We've got a claim. But the point is moot. NicolasNorth, LLC is incorporated in Delaware. Third Circuit, baby.

But aren't you going after Santa for the same sort of thing the Easter Bunny does?

How do you mean?

I mean the Easter Bunny's got that holiday locked up as tightly as Santa's got Christmas. If you go after Santa, you leave the Easter Bunny vulnerable to same restraint of trade argument. And then the next thing you know, you'll have an Easter Claus.

I think such speculation is wild and baseless and I can say with authority that the Easter Bunny welcomes any legitimate competition and would never in any way engage in the sort of illegal trade practice you allege. I'm shocked you would even suggest it. I can't believe I'm sitting with you now. If I had known your intent was to slander the Easter Bunny, I would have never let you through the door.

The Easter Bunny is listening to us now, isn't he.

This conversation is over.

JANGLE THE ELF
GRANTS WISHES

"You wanted to see me, boss?"

"Ah, Jangle. Come in, come in. Have a seat."

"Thank you, ma'am."

"You excited about Christmas this year, Jangle?"

"I always am, ma'am. It's our busiest time of the year, isn't it?"

"That it is. Just one day to go now."

"Believe me, I know it. It's crunch time down there on the floor. This is one worker bee who keeps flying with the nectar known as caffeine, if you know what I mean."

"Oh, I do."

"It's a lot of work, but what can I say? I love it here."

"Well, see, Jangle, that's what I need to talk to you about today."

"Ma'am?"

"Let me start by asking you this. What do you see as the purpose of our corporate division?"

"The Department of Non-Material Christmas Wishes?"

"Yes. Our little group. The one you worked so hard to transfer into six months ago."

"Oh, well, I mean, our job is to evaluate those wishes and, when possible, make those wishes come true."

"True as far as it goes. What else?"

"Well, out of all the divisions, we're the only ones that deliver our wishes early. Because when people wish for non-material things, they sometimes want for them to happen *before* Christmas so that they can then have a better Christmas."

"Also true, as far as it goes."

"Is…there a problem with my production on the Non-Material Wishes floor, ma'am? I know I'm new to the division, but I've been working really hard to clear acceptable requests. If you look at my record, you'll see I'm one of the top fulfillers of wishes this month."

"You are! And that in itself should be something to be commended."

"Thank you!"

"But, Jangle, your fulfilling these wishes is why I've called you in here today."

"I'm not sure I understand."

"Well, for example, this fulfilled wish that I have here in my hand. From Genevieve Wilson of Aurora, Illinois."

"I remember her wish. She asked for a white Christmas."

"And you gave it to her."

"Sure I did! Who doesn't love a white Christmas?"

"You gave her a white Christmas by creating a massive snowstorm that dumped eighteen to twenty-four inches of snow in twenty-four hours across four states in the Midwest."

"See, I figured there would be other people in those states who were hoping for a white Christmas too. So I cleared the board for everyone in Non-Material Wishes. Cut their workload."

"You also shut down the airports in Chicago and Denver."

"Oh…well, that will be cleared up soon, I'm sure."

"A hundred thousand homes in Wisconsin without power."

"A perfect time for families to snuggle by the fire. We're bringing them together."

"Interstates 80 *and* 90 closed, snarled interstate commerce at Christmas and thousands stranded on the roads in their cars."

"Look, all of that is an *infrastructure* problem, isn't it? I can't be blamed for them not funding their transportation system."

"Let's move on to another fulfilled wish. Timmy Washington wanted his brother, in the Army, home for Christmas."

"And I got him there!"

"You put grenade shrapnel in his butt to do it!"

"Hey, *you* try getting the military to allow quick turnaround leave. And anyway, he's eligible for a Purple Heart now."

"Not for a wound gained while he was sweeping up the armory at his Army base in Arkansas."

"Are you sure?"

"I'm sure."

"Well, that doesn't seem fair at all."

"What doesn't seem fair is that now Timmy's brother won't be able to *sit* for six weeks."

"Okay, well, if we're going to quibble over *details*—"

"Cassie Anderson! Wants her mom to be happy this Christmas!"

"Did you read that file? It's heartbreaking! Her mom deserves happiness!"

"And you gave it to her by slipping her an entire platter of pot brownies?!?"

"'Slipping' is not the way I'd put it. I just made sure there was a mix-up at the PTA bake sale."

"You can't go around *drugging* people, Jangle."

"Her mom is pretty happy right now."

"*Stoned* is not the same as *happy*."

"Maybe not the way *you* do it."

"Jangle—"

"Every pot brownie I've ever had made me positively *giddy*."

"*Jangle*. Look—okay, maybe I'm going about this wrong. Tell me, have you ever heard of 'The Monkey's Paw?'"

"Sure, it's a monkey's little furry hand."

"No, I mean the story."

"Someone did a story about a monkey's hand?"

"A paw. A monkey's paw. The paw was cursed."

"Who would curse a monkey?"

"Not the whole monkey, just its paw."

"I mean, I feel like if one part of your body is cursed, you're sort of *generally* cursed, don't you?"

"For goodness sake, the paw wasn't on the monkey anymore!"

"What? What happened to the rest of the monkey?"

"It doesn't matter! The point is the paw was cursed."

"I'd think this poor amputee monkey would certainly think so."

"Forget about the monkey! This is about the paw!"

"How did the paw get cursed anyway?"

"In the story, an old Indian fakir cursed it."

"Okay, see, now, that's just racist."

"Jangle! The point is that when people made wishes on the paw, the wishes would come true…in the worst possible way. Just like what you're doing."

"You're saying I'm using the monkey's paw?"

"I'm saying you *are* the monkey's paw."

"So now I'm cursed by an Indian religious ascetic?!?"

"Oh, for the love of Pete! It has nothing to do with any religious ascetic of any nationality!"

"Then who's cursed me?"

"No one has cursed you! It's a metaphor!"

"About being cursed!"

"No! About not paying attention to the consequences of wishes!"

"Well…whatever. I'm still going to report this conversation to HR. It's gone to some really weird and uncomfortable places, if you ask me."

"Oh for— *Look*. Jangle. All I am asking you to do is pay a little more attention to *how* you're granting people's wishes.

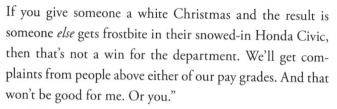

If you give someone a white Christmas and the result is someone *else* gets frostbite in their snowed-in Honda Civic, then that's not a win for the department. We'll get complaints from people above either of our pay grades. And that won't be good for me. Or you."

"Hmmm. I see your point, ma'am."

"So no more winter storms or shrapnel?"

"Fine. Although I still stand by the pot brownies."

"We can discuss that one another time. But I appreciate your willingness to work with me here, Jangle."

"You're welcome, ma'am. May I go back to my desk now? I still have some wishes to clear by the end of the day."

"You can. What's the one you're working on now?"

"I have a five-year-old asking for world peace."

"You're gonna have to pass on that one."

"I don't know. I think I can manage it."

"Without the use of a sudden global nuclear holocaust?"

"Of course!"

"*Or* a humanity-eradicating plague?"

"*Damn it.* Never mind."

SCRIPT NOTES ON THE
BIRTH OF JESUS

Dear Matt and Luke:

We just read through your story treatment of *The Birth of Jesus*. We love it. *Love* it. Seriously, "love" is not nearly the right word for what we feel about what will almost certainly become a perennial seasonal classic. I hope the two of you have made space for awards on your mantelpieces; I think it's about to get very crowded up there!

We've shared this important piece of work around, including with the marketing folks and our intern, Chad. While everyone agrees that your vision for this story is critical and elemental, we do have a few notes that we feel will help this film reach the audiences who so desperately need to hear its message, while at the same time staying true to this timeless tale. You'll find them below.

1. We're a little worried about the title. *The Birth of Jesus* has a vintage feel to it; we need something a little more four-quadrant, which will bring in audiences of all ages. How do you feel about *Christ: Origins?* It's punchy and gives us a template for sequels, if we go that route (*Christ: Dead Sea Rising* and *Christ: The Final Chapter* are two titles Chad suggested). Let us know.

2. Mary and Joseph are central characters and we love that they are clearly there for each other and involved with each other, no matter what. That's a real *Notebook*-like vibe that date night audiences really go for. But you don't give them a lot of dialogue that grounds their characters into their relationship. Can you punch up their scenes, give them some banter, and maybe inject some humor into it? A pregnancy and birth offer up a lot of opportunities for zany slapstick scenarios. Chad noted that *Juno* rode that basic idea to a screenplay Oscar, and he has a point. Think about it.

3. On that note: Channing Tatum as Joseph?

4. We were worried about the logistics of having a birth scene near a manger—it's a little *downmarket* for our audiences—until marketing pointed out this gives us an opportunity to create a line of stuffed animals timed to the film release. That really helps us with the 10-and-under audience.

With that in mind, please give thought to how we can incorporate into the birth scene a group of wisecracking, animatronic livestock, who comment on the action. Also think about how we can make the livestock extensible beyond plush toys. We're talking spin-off animated series and theme park characters here.

5. Chad's idea here: Ariana Grande as a baby lamb who is Jesus' first pal. Or even better: Sidekick! Then we can also get her to sing the movie theme song. We've got Charli XCX writing that. It's gonna be huge.

6. The angel announcing the birth of Jesus to the shepherds is a powerful scene, one that's really going to justify the CGI and 3D conversion. The thing we were wondering is why an angel—a supremely powerful creature—announces the birth of the single most important person in the world to...shepherds. We're just not seeing the utility there, and the shepherds don't really do much with the information.

Then Chad had a suggestion: What if the angel is secretly a *fallen* angel, and the shepherds aren't really shepherds at all, but a secret order of demon worshippers disguised as shepherds, who have been waiting for centuries, at the ready, to kidnap the savior foretold by prophecy at the moment of his birth, and the fallen angel is telling them so they can put their dark plan into action? Now, *that* makes sense! Even better, we can have the sheep they guard act as spies for the forces of good—the lamb played by Ariana Grande can race to the inn to tell the other livestock, who will then form a woolly shield around Jesus. I get a lump in my throat just thinking about it.

7. Video game idea—*Christ: Race to the Manger.* Let's talk to Electronic Arts about that.

8. This takes us to the Three Wise Men. Frankly, we were all a little confused by these characters. They sort of come out of nowhere and their reasons for offering up very expensive gifts are sketchy at best. So marketing and Chad spitballed it and came up with a couple of things we think you're going to love. One, the three wise men are not from The East—they're from The Future (which they call "The East" as future slang). Two, they've come from the future not just to give gifts, but to act as bodyguards for the baby Jesus against the demon-worshipping hordes. They are future ninjas for Christ.

Three, their gifts have changed slightly. One of them (who we see played by Idris Elba) brings a robot, who will teach Jesus about humanity and martial arts. The second one (Sarah Jessica Parker) will be bringing the traditional fragrances, only now they're from Chanel—marketing will work out the deal. The third (Jack Black) brings gold, because gold. The battle scene between the Awesome Jesus Ninja Triad (it's a zippier description, much better for action figure sales) and the demon-worshipping hordes is going to be spectacular; we're already negotiating with Yuen Woo-ping for the wire-fu scenes.

9. Also, to secure Chinese financing, we'll have to move the location of the birth from Bethlehem to Shanghai. I'm sure we can find a way to make this canonically sound.

10. The only problem with the demon worshippers vs Future Ninjas subplot is that by necessity it pushes Joseph and Mary out of the narrative frame a little more than we would like. The good news is once again our intern Chad has come up with an ingenious solution—what if Joseph isn't *really* the humble carpenter he's been portrayed as, but has also traveled even *further* back in time than the Awesome Jesus Ninja Triad, because he knows *they were defeated* by the demon-worshipping hordes, and that *he* is Mary and

Jesus' only hope of survival? So the visit to Bethlehem, the trip to the inn, the birth in the manger all set up the real story of the film: The final confrontation between Joseph, Warrior of the 37th century, and Asphalbelub, the fallen angel—who is *also* revealed to be secretly from the future, not to mention a Venusian/Murderbot hybrid.

(This is important because suddenly this story, previously magical—and let's face it, maybe a little *far-fetched*—is now grounded in actual science! Because time-traveling warriors and murderbot hybrids are *plausible* in a physical universe. This is like how George Lucas explained the Force with Midi-chlorians—and boy, that cleared up a lot of questions for everyone.)

Naturally, we need to work on the details, but according to Chad, it all ends up with Joseph defeating Asphalbelub, putting Mary and Jesus on his timechopper (cleverly disguised as the manger this whole time!) and returning to the 37th century, where Jesus learns fighting skills and matter manipulation from his robot guru before coming back down the time stream to take on the Romans, all of which leads up to the ultimate, final confrontation between him and Mecha-Caesar.

I think you'll agree these new elements really work to strengthen the story of Jesus' birth.

Also, we've made Chad a producer on the film.

Let us know what you think—after the new year, of course. We understand there are a few holidays to get through between now and then.

Yours,

Peter Stone, VP of Story Development

SARAH'S
SISTER

Sarah's family had just sat down for dinner when Mom said "uh-oh," and the next thing everyone knew was there was a huge gush of water. Mom had been big as a horse for two months, but the fact was the water breaking was early; she wasn't supposed to give birth until a couple of weeks into the new year. The family just wasn't prepared for a Christmas Eve baby; Mom hadn't gotten her hospital bag together yet, and Dad hadn't made the arrangements to make sure Sarah had someone to watch over her while the baby was being born. Although *that* might have had something to do with the fact Mom wanted her to be in the delivery room to watch it happen, a prospect that filled Sarah with queasy terror. She was ten, after all; she *knew* where babies came from. She wasn't at all sure she actually wanted to watch one being born.

They were so unprepared, in fact, that Mom and Dad hadn't even gotten around to giving the baby a name. Which boggled Sarah's mind. They had *months* to come up with something, and they even knew the baby was another girl. And yet Mom and Dad were still talking about it. They were talking about it just as Mom's water broke. Dad had been offering up names, stopped while the family said grace and then started up again right after as if he hadn't stopped at all. Even now, as he guided Mom into the minivan for the trip to the hospital, he was still at it.

"'Abigail,'" he said. "You like that name."

"I never said I liked that name," Mom said, as she wedged herself into the seat.

"'Cynthia,' then," Dad said. "Don't you have a cousin named 'Cynthia'?"

"I do," Mom said. "And I never liked her. She used to hit me at family picnics. She's awful."

"Maybe she's grown up to be a better person," Dad said, as he threw the quickly-assembled hospital bag into the back of the minivan.

"I don't think I'm willing to take that chance," Mom said, and then kind of fazed out for a second. "Whoo. Contraction. Less talk, Bill. More driving."

But Dad didn't stop throwing out names the entire trip to the hospital. He tried "Sandy," and "Cindy," "Jennifer," and "Martha," "Lesley" and "Linda" and "Liesel." The last one got Mom's attention.

"'Liesel?'" she said. "Are we going to be raising a new generation of Von Trapp children?"

"It's unusual," Dad reasoned.

"Yeah, and for a reason," Mom said, and then had another contraction. After it was done, she looked at Sarah in the rear-view mirror. "What do you think, Sarah?" she said. "Have any great ideas for a name for your sister?"

Sarah, in the second row of the minivan, shrugged. "I don't know," Sarah said. And she didn't. She'd been studiously avoiding thinking of a name for months now and didn't see a reason to start this minute. She looked away from her mom and out the window; from the corner of her eye she could see her mom still looking at her in the rear-view mirror before Dad piped up again and suggested the name "Courtney."

When Dad parked by the emergency room entrance and ran out to get a wheelchair, Mom turned around as much as possible to look at Sarah directly. "Hey, Sweets," she said, using Sarah's old nickname. "Are you okay? You don't look so happy."

Sarah shrugged again. "It's all right," she said. "It's just—"

"It's just that it's Christmas Eve and tonight we're supposed to be having fun with you, right?" Mom smiled. "I'm really sorry, Sweets. You're going to have to believe me that I wouldn't have chosen Christmas Eve to have a baby, either. But she's on her way. Sometimes we don't get to decide these things."

"I know, Mom," Sarah said. "It's okay."

"You know, Sarah," Mom said, "at my last appointment with Dr. Roth, I told her that I want you to be in the delivery room for the birth, and she said it would be okay. In fact, if you want, you can help your dad cut the umbilical cord. Do you think you'd like to do that?"

"I have to think about it," Sarah said, carefully.

"Okay, Sweets," Mom said, and then tensed up for another contraction. "Ow. Better hurry, girlie. These contractions are getting stronger. Your sister could be here any minute."

But she wasn't. Sarah's sister hadn't arrived at seven, eight or nine o'clock, and at ten o'clock Sarah noticed that her mom hadn't been talking much for the last hour, and neither Dad or Dr. Roth were talking much either, or smiling. In the last minutes before eleven, more doctors and nurses had come into the room to talk with Dr. Roth and Dad. Finally, at eleven, orderlies came in to wheel Mom out of the room. Dad whispered something to Mom, kissed her, and then turned to Sarah.

"Sarah," he said.

"Where are they taking Mom?" Sarah said.

Dad took Sarah's hand. "Sarah, the baby is having trouble coming out," he said. "They have to take Mom to an operating room."

"Is she going to be all right?" Sarah asked.

"She'll be fine," Dad said, rushing through the words. "She'll be fine. The baby should be fine, too. But you can't be in the room with her now. There are going to be too many doctors and nurses in the room with your mother. I'm going to call your grandparents to come and get you, okay?"

Sarah nodded. Without another word, Dad took Sarah into the maternity waiting room, sat her down in a chair, and went over to the pay phone on the wall to call Sarah's grandparents. Sarah watched her dad make the call; he was turned away from her and hunched over the phone receiver. He talked very quietly into the phone. Sarah couldn't hear what he said. After a few minutes he put the phone back on the hook and came over to Sarah.

"They'll be here in about an hour," Dad said. "Maybe a little longer depending on the weather. I'll stay with you until then."

Sarah looked up at her dad. "I think Mom needs you, Dad," she said. "You should be with her."

"I can't leave you alone, honey," Dad said.

"I'm fine, Dad," Sarah said, and pointed at the reception desk. "There's a nurse there. Nothing's going to happen to me. I'll be perfectly all right until Grandma and Grandpa get here."

Dad looked down the hallway, to where Mom was wheeled away. "Are you sure you'll be okay?" he said.

"I'll be, fine, Dad, really," Sarah said. "Go be with Mom."

Dad suddenly dropped to his knees and gave Sarah a fierce hug. "I love you, Sarah," he said, and when he pulled back so Sarah could see his face, she could see that he was about to cry. "I love you very much. You don't forget it."

"I won't," Sarah said. Dad got up and started walking down the hall. Near the end of the hall, he began to jog.

Sarah looked around the maternity waiting room. It was utterly empty. From end to end, she was the only person in it. In one far corner, a TV sat, on mute, with *A Christmas Story* playing. On the other far side of the room was the reception desk. A nurse sat there, flipping through a magazine. She looked up at Sarah and gave her a small smile. Sarah smiled back and then looked away quickly, and then watched *A Christmas Story*, with the sound off, for she didn't know how long.

Sarah eventually became thoroughly bored. She got up to get a drink from the water fountain by the pay phone. As she reached out to the water fountain, a small spark leapt from her finger to the fountain (or maybe the other way around, she wasn't sure). *Zap.* Static electricity. It hurt, but it was interesting. Sarah began walking around the waiting room, scuffling her feet as she went. Every few seconds she'd reach out and touch something metal. A chair. *Zap.* The fire extinguisher container. *Zap.* The cord on the pay phone. *Zap.* After a couple minutes of this, she figured she'd built up an immunity to the pain. She made an entire circuit around the waiting area, scuffling her feet all the way, and then reached out to the water fountain.

ZAP!

Sarah snatched back her hand and waved it from the wrist, grimacing with her eyes closed and hopping on one foot. That *really* hurt. After a minute of this she opened her eyes again.

A boy was standing in the room with her. He looked to be her age, or maybe a little bit older. He was wearing a brown sweater and blue jeans, and had brown hair and eyes. His nose was really big for his face. He was looking at her curiously.

"What are you looking at?" Sarah said.

"I was looking at you," the boy said. "I was wondering what you were doing."

"I wasn't doing anything," Sarah said. "Mind your own business."

"I'm sorry," the boy said. "I didn't mean to make you angry."

"I'm not angry," Sarah said. "I just hurt myself. I got shocked really hard."

"How did that happen?" the boy asked.

Sarah narrowed her eyes. "I did it on purpose, okay? Are you happy now?"

"I was just asking," the boy said. "It gets kind of boring around here. You looked like you were having fun."

Sarah blinked. She had been feeling herself rolling into a bad mood, and she was using this boy to get there; suddenly he'd derailed her. "Who are you?" she asked.

"I'm Josh," he said, and stuck out his hand. After a minute Sarah took it.

Zap.

Josh grinned. "Static electricity," he said. He sat down in one of the chairs. His feet swayed back and forth, like pendulum.

"So why are you here?" Sarah asked him.

"I'm waiting for my dad," Josh said. "I was in another part of the hospital but I decided to take a walk. Why are you here?"

"My mom's having a baby," Sarah said.

"On Christmas Eve?" Josh said. "Wow. That's cool."

Sarah shrugged. "I guess," she said. She slumped into the seat next to him and began kicking her feet as well.

"I think it would neat to have a birthday on Christmas Eve," Josh said.

"I wouldn't," Sarah said. "It's too close to Christmas. Everybody would give you gifts and say 'Happy birthday and merry Christmas'. What a rip-off."

"Maybe," Josh said. "But you'd also have your birthday when there were all those lights and people were happy and singing carols and stuff. That's not so bad."

"As long as you liked carols," Sarah said. "Maybe if you heard carols being sung around your birthday for your whole life you'd get sick of them. Some of those carols are really bad, anyway."

"Which ones?" Josh asked.

"'Twelve Days of Christmas,'" Sarah said. "I hate it. And no one knows what comes after 'five golden rings.'"

"Six geese a-laying," Josh said.

"Okay, *you* know," Sarah said, testily. "But no one else does. And just imagine having to hear it every single time your birthday comes around."

"I never thought of it that way," Josh said. "But you know, everyone hears that 'Happy Birthday' song on their birthday and no one ever gets sick of *that*."

Sarah gave Josh a skeptical look.

"All right, maybe that's a bad example," Josh admitted.

"Ha!" Sarah said. She gave her feet an extra, triumphant swing.

Josh stood up. "There's a cafeteria down the hall," he said. "It's closed, but there's vending machines. Want to go get something?"

Sarah looked around. "I don't think I should leave," she said. "My grandparents are on their way."

"It's not far. We'll be able to hear them," Josh said.

"I don't have any money," Sarah said.

"My treat," Josh said.

Sarah was about to say no, but then her stomach rumbled and she remembered that they didn't actually have dinner that night. "Okay," she said. "But we have to come right back."

"Deal," Josh said, and they took off down the hall. The vending machines were where they were promised. Sarah got a Snickers bar and an apple juice; Josh got powdered donuts and grape juice. They sat at a table in the cafeteria and ate. Sarah tore through her candy bar and gulped through her juice; she hadn't realized just how hungry she'd been. Josh ate slowly. After she was finished with her candy bar, Sarah looked over to Josh.

"Do you have any brothers or sisters?" Sarah asked.

"No," Josh said. "I'm an only child. What about you?"

"I'm an only child, too," Sarah said. "Well. Was an only child. Now I'll have a sister."

"I've always wanted a sister," Josh said. "Or a brother. I'd like to have either."

"Why?" Sarah asked. "My friend Angela has a brother who is two years younger than her. They're always fighting. Every time I go over to her house, her brother is always doing something rotten to her and picking fights with her. And then their mother comes in and yells at them both. None of them ever seem to get along."

"Not every family does that," Josh said.

"A lot of them do," Sarah said.

"You'll be a lot older than your sister," Josh said. "Maybe you won't have anything to fight about."

Sarah thought about that. She *would* be a lot older than her sister. When the kid was in kindergarten, Sarah would already be in high school. They probably wouldn't fight; in fact, she would probably be helping Mom with things instead of getting into it with her sister.

"Hello?" Josh said. "You kind of zoned out there."

"Huh?" Sarah said. "I was just thinking about my mom."

"What about her?" Josh asked.

"I was just thinking about how my mom always wanted another baby," Sarah said. "I remember, there were a couple of times where she thought she was going to have a baby, only she didn't."

"What happened?" Josh asked.

"She had miscarriages," Sarah said. "You know what those are, right?" Josh nodded. "Well, anyway. I remember the first time she had one. She had to go to the hospital and then when she came home, she cried all night long. I remember waking up in the middle of the night and hearing her cry."

"What did you do?" Josh asked.

"What do mean, what did I do?" Sarah said. "I wasn't supposed to be awake. I just stayed in bed and then I went back to sleep. That was that time. Then she had another miscarriage about a year later. She didn't cry when it happened that time. She was just sad."

"It's a sad thing," Josh said.

"And when she got pregnant this time, she and Dad didn't tell anyone about it until she was showing," Sarah said. "She didn't even tell *me*."

"Maybe she was worried about it," Josh said.

"Talking about it isn't going to make anything bad happen," Sarah shot back.

"I know," Josh said. "But maybe after two times, she didn't want to get anyone's hopes up. Maybe especially hers."

"You don't know anything," Sarah said, hotly. "You've never even met my mom. You don't know why she didn't tell anyone."

"We could go say hi," Josh said, after a minute.

"What?" Sarah said.

"The delivery rooms are right down this hall," Josh said. "We could go say hi. They'd let you in."

"Don't be *stupid*," Sarah said. "She's giving birth. I'm not just going to go in and say hello. She's kind of busy. Besides, she's not there. She's in an operating room."

"Oh," Josh said.

"*Oh*," Sarah mocked back. She looked down at her candy bar wrapper. She was still hungry.

"Here," Josh said, and passed her the donut package. "Take these." Sarah reached over to take them. A small spark shot from her hand to Josh's as they touched. "Sorry," Josh said.

"It's all right," Sarah said. "Thank you." She took one of the little donuts and took a bite, but her mouth was too dry to swallow. She looked over to Josh again. He smiled and passed over his grape juice.

"I'm eating all your stuff," Sarah said after she was able to swallow.

"It's all right," Josh said. "I don't mind sharing. Is your mom going to be okay?"

"My dad said she was going to be fine," Sarah said. "And the baby too. But…" Sarah trailed off.

"You think he lied to you," Josh said. "To keep you from being worried."

Sarah nodded. "He doesn't lie very well. When I turned eight he was supposed to not tell me I was getting a surprise birthday party. He did such a bad job of it I finally told him that I could tell he was lying about it."

"I bet he didn't like that," Josh said.

Sarah laughed. "No. But it was okay. I pretended to be surprised when we got home. I didn't want him to get in trouble with Mom." At the mention of her mom, Sarah got silent again and stared down at the remaining donut in the package. She suddenly wasn't very hungry at all.

"Hey," Josh said. "Are you okay?"

"I'm fine," Sarah said.

Josh looked at her for a minute. Then he stood up. "Come on," he said to her, holding out his hand. "I want to show you something."

"What?" Sarah asked.

"It's a surprise," Josh said. "It's not too far away. We'll still be able to hear your grandparents when they come in. But I think it might cheer you up."

Sarah looked up at him, then reached out to take his hand. Another spark zapped between them. "Sorry," Josh said, and grinned. With her hand in his, Josh and Sarah left the cafeteria and walked down the hall, into the maternity ward.

"Here we are," Josh said, and stopped in front of a large window. On the other side of the window were five newborn babies, three boys and two girls.

Sarah looked over at Josh. "Why did you bring me here?" she asked. "Why would I want to look at babies?"

"Because they're babies," Josh said, looking through the window. "They're brand new to the world. Just look at them. Babies always cheer me up when I'm sad."

"I never said I was sad," Sarah said.

Josh looked over to Sarah.

She shrugged defensively. "I'm not sad. I'm worried," she said.

Josh tapped the glass, lightly, and looked back in. "*They're* not worried," he said. "It's too early for them to be worried, or sad, or upset. The worst thing that happens to a baby is being hungry."

"You could have a wet diaper," Sarah said.

"I suppose," Josh said. "But no matter what, it doesn't last long. Your mom or dad come in to feed you or change you and help you get back to sleep. It's easier to be happy when you're a baby."

Sarah looked at the baby closest to her. *Baby Baker,* the small sign on her bed read. *Six pounds, four ounces. 18 inches. It's a girl!*

"They're so small," Sarah said.

"They have to be," Josh said. "You know, to come out…" Josh shut up quickly.

"I know where babies come from," Sarah said. "My parents had that talk with me."

"It's weird to think that one day all these babies will be as big as we are," Josh said. "Can you remember being that small?"

"No," Sarah said. "The first thing I remember was when I was two and petting the cat. What's the first thing you remember?"

"My mother," Josh said. "I remember waking up from a nap and seeing her smiling down at me. And I remember being happy to see her. It's nice to be a baby, and know how much you're loved."

"It's nice to be a baby," Sarah said. She turned back to look at the little girl in front of her. It was only after the first tear fell that she noticed she was crying.

There was a muffled click. Josh looked up at the clock above the window. "Midnight," he said. "It's Christmas now."

Sarah sobbed loudly, and sat down hard on the floor underneath the window. She pulled in her knees tight and covered her face with her hands. "I'm sorry," she said. "I'm sorry, I'm sorry, oh God, I'm so sorry."

Josh came over to her. "Hey," he said. "Hey. Why are you sorry? What did you do?"

"I didn't want my mom to get pregnant," Sarah said, gulping the words from between her palms. "I never wanted her to become pregnant. And each time she miscarried I knew she was sad, but I *wasn't*. And this time, when they found out it was a girl, they kept thinking up names and asking me to think up names and I wouldn't. I didn't want a sister. And I wished…" Sarah started crying again.

Josh gently reached up and took one of Sarah's hands. "What did you wish for, Sarah?" he asked.

Sarah looked at Josh. "I wished she would go away. My sister. I didn't know how. I didn't want my mom to be sad. But I just wished she would *go*. And now my mother's in an operating room and I don't know what's going to happen to her and I don't know what's going to happen to the baby and the only thing I can think about is how *sorry* I am for wishing she'd go away. I *don't* want her to go. I *don't* want this to happen. I *don't* want this." She took her hand back from Josh and covered her face again. "I'm so sorry I ever wanted this. I'm so sorry."

Josh put his arm around Sarah, there on the floor, and let her cry. Then after Sarah mostly stopped crying, Josh said. "You never asked for this to happen."

"I wished for her to go away," Sarah said.

"But you never asked for it to happen this way," Josh said. "You never asked for harm to come to your mom or to your sister. You just wished she wouldn't happen. But she'd already happened. You said your mom didn't tell you about your sister until she was sure as she could be that she was on her way. And you couldn't have changed that, Sarah. No matter how hard you wished. This isn't your fault."

"I still feel bad, though," Sarah said. "I still *hurt.*"

"I know," Josh said. "I can see that. But I think I know a way to make it stop hurting."

"How?" Sarah asked.

"Come on," Josh said, and stood up. "Stand up." He held out his hand to her, she took it. There was a little electric shock between them but this time neither of them said anything about it. Josh helped Sarah get to her feet and then turned her around to look at the babies.

"Look at them," Josh said. "Soon they're going to go back to their mothers. And their mothers are going to see them and hold them and love them. But you know what I think. I think the mothers loved them already. From the instant they knew they were there, they loved them, and they loved them more than anything else in the world. And it's not just the mother who loved them. It's the father, the sisters and brothers, the whole family. A baby comes into the world already loved by those who are waiting for it to be born. You know?"

"Yes," Sarah whispered, as she looked at the babies. "Yes. It's true."

"You've been holding back, Sarah," Josh said. "All the love that you have for your sister. Because I think it's there. I know it. I can see it by looking at you. You've never not loved her, Sarah. You've just been trying to keep it locked away, to hide it from her, and to keep it from yourself. And it hurts not to give her that love. It hurts not to let it out."

"Yes," Sarah said again. "It does hurt."

"So let it out, Sarah," Josh said. "All that love you've been hiding. Let it out. All of it. Right now. Let her know you've loved her from the minute you knew she was coming. And never stop. Never stop loving her for as long as you live."

Sarah sobbed again, and held a hand to the glass. "My sister," she said. "I do. I do love her. I do. I love her so much. I do."

"I know," Josh said. "*She* knows."

Sarah turned to Josh and hugged him fiercely and cried into his shoulder. Josh held her back and stroked her hair. They stayed that way for a while.

Eventually Sarah broke her hug and stepped back from Josh. He was smiling. "How do you feel?" he asked.

Sarah gave a small, surprised laugh. "Better," she said, and then looked into his face. "Better. A lot better."

"Come on," Josh said. "You should get back to the waiting room."

They walked down the hall and back into the waiting room. Sarah went to the bathroom to wash off her face. When she came back out, she looked at Josh. "My grandparents should be here soon," she said. "Let's sit until they get here."

"I have to go," Josh said. "My father's been calling to me, I'm sure."

"But I want you to meet my sister," Sarah said. "You can't go now."

"I have to," Josh said. "I'm sorry. But I was wondering if you could give her something from me."

"Okay," Sarah said. "What is it?"

Josh came over the Sarah, and with an awkward little smile, gave her a kiss on the cheek. As he did so, a little spark went from his lips to her cheek. Sarah held her cheek, as much in surprise of the kiss as to register the shock.

"Static electricity," Sarah said, and smiled. She felt giddy and a little embarrassed.

"Goodbye, Sarah," Josh said. "I'm glad we met. Don't forget to give that to your sister."

"I won't," Sarah said. "Goodbye, Josh. Thank you."

Josh waved. Then he wandered down the hall and out of sight. As he did, Sarah saw her grandparents emerge from the outside, looking around the waiting room for her. She waved to them and began walking over to them. About halfway to them, though she noticed their attention was suddenly somewhere else. She turned around and saw her father.

"Dad!" she said and ran to him. She stopped when she saw his face. For the very first time in her life, she saw her father as old.

"Hey, Dad," Sarah said.

Dad looked down at Sarah, reached out to her, hugged her hard enough to squeeze air out of her, and kissed the top of her head. "Hello, baby," he said, finally.

"Is everything okay?" Sarah asked.

Dad broke his hug and looked down at Sarah. "Sarah, could you do something for me? I need to talk to your grandparents for a minute. Would you sit down while I talk to them?"

"Sure, Dad," Sarah said.

"Thank you, Sarah," Dad said. Sarah went and sat while Dad went up to Sarah's grandparents. Sarah could see Dad, Grandma and Grandpa huddle in close. Then Grandma put her hand to her mouth; Grandpa quickly walked her over to a seat. Dad looked at them for a few moments, then turned around to Sarah. He came over and sat down next to her.

"How are you doing, baby?" Dad asked.

"I'm okay," Sarah said.

"Sarah," Dad said. "I have to tell you something. Your mother had some problems with the birth."

"Is Mom okay?" Sarah asked.

"Mom is fine, baby," Dad said. "She's fine. She's all right. But—" Dad's face suddenly tightened. He took in air in a gasp.

"But the baby's not all right," Sarah said.

Dad shook his head, looked away, and took another deep breath. "No," he said. "No. The doctors tried to help her. But they couldn't. I'm sorry, Sarah. I'm sorry."

Sarah thought for a minute, silent. "Where is she now?" Sarah finally asked.

"The doctors are letting your mother have a few minutes with her," Dad said.

"I want to see her," Sarah said.

"Oh, honey," Dad said. "Honey. I don't know."

"I want to see her," Sarah said, insistent. "She's my sister. I'll never get to see her again. Please, Dad. Please. She's my sister. Let me see my sister."

Dad's face twisted up again, and he put his hands over his eyes and cried for a few seconds. Then he stood up and without a word held out his hand for Sarah to take. And then he took her to the room her mother was in.

Her mother lay on a bed, pale. In her arms was a small and almost indistinct bundle of blankets. Sarah and Dad stood in the doorway, silent, until Mom looked over and saw them there.

"Hey, Sweets," Mom said, in the smallest voice Sarah had ever heard her use. She took one arm and held it out to Sarah. "Come here, baby."

Sarah went to her mother and took her hand. Mom gripped Sarah's hand, hard.

"Is this her?" Sarah asked.

"Yes, Sweets," Mom said. "It's her. It's your sister."

"I'm sorry, Mom," Sarah said. "I really am."

"So am I, baby," Mom said, and cried a little. "But it's all right. I have you. I have your father. We have each other. We have all the love we need," she said, and then held Sarah's hand to her cheek and cried a little bit more. "I'm all right," she finally said.

"Mom," Sarah said. "Mom, I'd like to hold her."

Mom looked at Sarah, concerned. "Baby," she said. "Are you sure?"

"I'm sure," Sarah said. "I'd like to hold her. Please, Mother."

Mom looked at Dad; Sarah looked over just in time to see him nod. Mom propped herself up a little, and carefully brought the bundle to Sarah's arms. Sarah took it and peered down and for the first time saw her sister, small and silent.

Oh, Sarah thought, and felt the love she'd held back so long come flooding out of her in a wild release. *Oh, my sister. Here you are, and all I can think about now are all the things I want to do for you. To hold you. To help you grow. To share the world with you. To share your joys and ease your pains. To do what I can to make the world worth having you in it. So many things I want to do. I wish I could. I wish.*

"I wish," Sarah said, and with those words smiled down at her sister.

"I love you, little sister," Sarah said. "I've loved you since the moment I knew you were coming to us. I love you, here in my arms. I will love you all my life. I love you, little sister. I give you my love."

Sarah bent, and gently kissed her sister's cheek. A little spark went from Sarah's lips to her sister's cheek. Static electricity, perhaps.

Sarah looked over at her mother, who was watching her with tears in her eyes. "I love you, Mom," Sarah said. She turned to her father. "I love you, Dad," she said.

Dad came over to Sarah, lifted her gently so as not to disturb the bundle she held, and placed her gently on her mother's bed. And then the family came together, all of them: Mother, father, Sarah and Sarah's sister. One family, one whole family, for the first time.

And it was there that Sarah felt the tiny breath on the tips of her fingers, curled in as they were near her sister's head. Then another and another, each breath only a little more forceful than the next until finally a cry came, and another and another, and then Dad was bursting off the bed to get a doctor and Mom was laughing and crying at the same time as she took her youngest daughter back into her arms and Sarah, well, all Sarah could do was take her mother's free hand, hold it to her and cry, cry into her mother's hand.

The week passed faster than anyone expected. There were tests, of course, but Sarah's sister was fine. There wasn't a thing wrong with her, Dr. Roth told Sarah's mom, and that was just fine with her. Now it was time for the whole family to go home and start being a family. And so Sarah and Dad brought the tiny new car seat, and while Dad placed the wriggling baby in it, Sarah helped her mom pack up her toiletries into her bag. Then down to the minivan and home, with Dad suggesting names all the way.

"Diana," he said. "Goddess of the moon. That's not a bad one."

"She's not a moon person," Mom said.

"Oh, and you can tell that," Dad said.

"Of course I can," Mom said. "I'm her mother."

"Well, we have to name her something," Dad said. "A whole week without a name is too long. And we've got a house packed with relatives right now. They're going to want to call her *something*."

Mom turned back to look at Sarah, riding in the seat next to her sister. "How about you, Sweets?" Mom said. "What do you think?"

Sarah looked over at her sister. She smiled. "Grace," Sarah said. "She's Grace."

Mom turned to Dad. "Well?" she said.

"Oh, I like that," Dad said. "I like it a lot."

"Grace," Mom said. "It's perfect, Sarah. It really is. What made you choose that?"

Sarah looked at her mom, and then back at her sister and held out a finger. Grace grabbed with her tiny hand. Sarah smiled.

"I didn't choose Grace," Sarah said. "It just came to me."

AN INTERVIEW WITH THE
NATIVITY INNKEEPER

Your name, please.

Ben Cohen.

Occupation?

Retired. I was an innkeeper.

In Bethlehem.

Right.

And in fact it was your inn where Jesus was born.

That's right. Well, not in the inn itself. Out back.

In the animal shed.

Yeah. I still get a lot of flak for that.

How do you mean?

I mean that people still criticize me for not having room at the inn. They say to me, you couldn't give a pregnant woman a room? You couldn't give a room to the woman pregnant with the divine child? Couldn't even spare a broom closet for the Baby Jesus?

How do you respond to that?

I say, well, look. First off, it wasn't just me. If you go back you'll see that every inn was full.

Because of the census.

Census, schmensus. It was the foot races. Bethlehem versus Cana. Also there was a touring theater troupe from Greece. Only appearance in Judea. The city was packed. We had reservations for months.

But Mary was pregnant.

I had three pregnant ladies at the inn that night. One was giving birth when Joe and Mary showed up. She was down the hall, screaming at the top of her lungs, cursing like you wouldn't believe. Her husband tried to encourage her to push and she kicked him in the groin. Think about that. She's crowning a baby, and she takes the time to put her foot into her husband's testicles. So maybe you'll understand why even if I had a room, I wouldn't be in a rush to give it up to those two.

But you ended up letting them go out to the animal shed.

That was an accident.

How so?

Joe comes in and asks for a room, and I tell him we're all out of rooms and have been for months. Foot races. Theater groupies. And such. And he says, come on, please. I've got a pregnant lady with me. And I say, you hear that down the hall? I'm full up with pregnant ladies. And he says, this baby is important. And I say, hey, buddy, I don't care if he's the Son of God, I don't have any rooms.

So there's some irony there.

I guess so. And then he says, look, we'll take anything. And so I say, as a joke, all right, you can go and sleep with animals if you like. And he says fine and slaps some money on the counter.

He called your bluff.

Yeah. And I say, I was kidding about that. And he says, my wife's water just broke in your lobby. What could I do? I pointed him in the direction of the animals.

It's better than having the baby in the street.

I suppose so, but you know, if the reason they were in Bethlehem was because of the census, then he had family in the area, right? It's his ancestral home and all that. He can't say to a cousin, hey, give us a couch? There are some family dynamics going on there that have been conveniently left unexamined, if you ask me.

Joseph had a lot on his mind.

Must have.

So the baby is born, and they place him in the manger.

Which, by the way, I told them not to do.

Why?

Because how unsanitary is that? Do you know what a manger is?

As far as I know, it's the place you put infant messiahs.

It's a food trough for animals.

Oh. Interesting.

"Oh, interesting" is right. Let me ask you. So your baby is born, and the first thing you do is put him in an open container filled with grain and covered in oxen drool? Does this seem reasonable to you?

You did have them out with the animals. Their options were limited.

I rented cribs. I asked Joseph, do you want a crib. And he said, no, we're fine, and then sets the kid in the food box. And I say to him, you're new at this, aren't you.

In his defense, he was.

And then someone says, look, the animals, they are adoring the baby. And I say, adoring, hell. They're wondering why there's a baby in their food.

On the other hand, the image of the Baby Jesus in the manger is a classic one.

Yeah, I mention that when people get on my case about not giving Joe and Mary a room. I tell them that having a Christmas carol called "Away in a Hotel Room" doesn't have quite the same ring to it. They never have anything to say to that.

It's said that a star appeared on the night when Jesus was born. Did you see it?

No. I was too busy trying to convince Joseph to rent a crib.

It's said it was bright enough to lead the Three Wise Men to your inn.

Well, three men showed up at the inn. I don't know how wise they were.

How do you mean?

The baby is born, right? And then these guys show up. And they say, we have brought gifts for the child. And I say, that's nice, what did you bring. And they say, we have brought gold and frankincense and myrrh. And I say, you've got to be kidding.

What's wrong with that?

Let me quote another Christmas song for you. "A child, a child, shivers in the cold, let us bring him silver and gold." Really? Silver and gold? And not, oh, I don't know, a blanket? An newborn infant is exhibiting signs of possible hypothermia and your response is to give him cold metal objects? Who ever wrote that song needs a smack upside the head.

You're saying the gifts were inappropriate.

What's wrong with diapers? A nice jumper or two? A Baby Bjorn? They were riding around on a donkey, you know. A Baby Bjorn would have come in handy. Have you ever in your life gone to a baby shower where someone says, congratulations on the baby, here's some perfume. No. Because most people have some sense.

I think the idea is that all the gifts were fit for a king.

Yes, a king who first pooped in my animals' manger. I would have appreciated a gift of diapers.

Point taken.

And another thing, they brought all these expensive gifts, but do you ever hear about Joe and Mary and Jesus being anything but poor? Or at the very most working class?

Now that you mention it, no.

Exactly. I think what happened is these three guys show up and they say, here are all these expensive gifts we got your baby. Oh and by the way, we happen to know King Herod thinks your baby's a threat and plans to kill every kid younger than two years of age just to be sure, so you better go. Egypt's nice this time of year. What? You're traveling by donkey? Well, then you can't take all these nice gifts with you. We'll just hold on to them for now, write us a letter when you get settled and we'll mail them. And then they never do.

I don't think there's scriptural support for that theory.

I'm not saying I have any evidence. All I'm saying is that it makes sense.

After the Three Wise Men, were there other visitors?

Yeah. It got a little crowded. The animal sheds aren't designed for a large amount of foot traffic. And then that kid showed up with a drum, and I said, all right, fine, we're done.

The song of that incident suggests the drum went over well.

Let me ask you. You're a parent, your child has just been born, he's tired, you're tired, people won't leave you alone, and then some delinquent comes by and unloads a snare solo in your baby's ear. Does this go over well?

Probably not, no.

There you go.

After the birth, did your inn benefit from the notoriety?

Not really. Jesus kind of slipped off everyone's radar, for, what? Thirty years? Thirty-five?

Something like that.

Right. So there wasn't much benefit there. I got some mileage out of telling the story about the crazy couple who rented my animal shed, and the visitors, and the drumming, but I mostly told it to friends. Then just as I'm about to retire someone tells me of this hippie preacher in Jerusalem who got in trouble with the Romans. And I say, hey, I think I know that guy. I think he got born in my shed. And then, well. You know what the Romans did to him.

Yes.

Romans, feh. Then I sold the inn to my nephew and retired to Joppa. By the time Jesus became really famous I was out of the game. And then my nephew sold the inn and they put that church there.

The Church of the Nativity.

You been?

I have, yes.

It's nice. I liked the inn better, of course.

Looking back, would you have done anything differently?

I would have comped Joseph the crib.

That still would have changed the Christmas carol.

I know. But, look. You didn't have to wash out that manger.

RESOLUTIONS FOR THE NEW YEAR:
A BULLET
POINT LIST

This next year, I resolve:

- **To lose weight**
  - Without considering lopping off a limb, which only works a few times
  - Or pretending kilograms are the same things as pounds, they're really not
  - Or coming up with a clone whose only job is to slap cheese out of my hands, how annoying would that be
  - And without causing a robotic revolution that destroys human civilization so that the only things

around to eat are rats and earthworms and possibly Chuck, that annoying dude from accounting

- **To exercise more**
  - And no, lifting nachos to one's mouth does not count as exercise, no matter if they are described as "loaded" or not
  - We're talking, like, actual walking or maybe even running
  - Actually this is where fomenting the robotic revolution would come in handy, running from murderous drones is SUPER cardio
  - I don't have to be the fastest runner after all, I just have to be faster than Chuck
  - Lol Chuck, he's got that bad knee, he's doomed

- **Go socialize more**
  - As in actually socialize more with actual live humans, not just snark on social media
  - Social media brings out my worst side, I'm bitter like three-day-old coffee
  - And anyway it's time to start hanging out with friends again
  - I mean, the friends who stayed with me after the breakup
  - After Kate left me
  - For Chuck
  - Goddamnit Chuck you suck

- **Start dating again**
  - I mean it's been like ten months since Kate left me, it's totally time
  - And all those dating apps make it easier to find someone
  - Someone like Kate, she was great
  - She smelled like flowers and vanilla

- **Buy more air freshener in flowers and vanilla scent**
  - That's probably not actually something that should be a resolution
  - It's more like a grocery list thing
  - And it won't replace Kate any way, it's just, like, chemicals
  - Damn it, Kate, why

- **TAKE FOLLICLES FROM THE HAIR BRUSH KATE LEFT AND CLONE HER**
  - No no no don't do that that's not the mature way of dealing with separation
  - Also kind of creepy
  - Also remember what happened the last time I tried something like that
  - Who knew there were federal regulations about cloning
  - I promised the USDA AND the NIH I wouldn't do that again
  - Damn it, focus on productive healthy new year's resolutions

- **BUILD THAT MURDER ROBOT TO TAKE OUT CHUCK FROM ACCOUNTING**
  - YEAH DIE CHUCK DIE HA HA HA HAH HA HAH
  - No wait
  - See, this is kind of the problem isn't it
  - I'm the one that drove Kate away with my monologues about robot uprisings and clones
  - Chuck probably never talks to her about either
  - He probably, I don't know, talks to her about her feelings and stuff
  - And validates her sense of self-worth
  - And is a really tender lover
  - GODDAMN IT CHUCK

- **Build a robot that DOESN'T murder Chuck but maybe, like, pokes him *real hard* in his bad knee when he isn't expecting it**
  - Baby steps toward a heathy response to Chuck in Accounting
  - And the fact he's probably a better person than I am
  - Although he's also probably never either cloned something or built a robot for any purpose, much less one that can poke knees like a freakin' *ninja*
  - Lol Chuck you suck
  - Okay stop thinking about Chuck get back to some sensible resolutions

- **Eat more green things**
  - Like leafy vegetables, to be clear
  - Not things with mold on them
  - You've been down *that* road before, it wasn't great
  - After Kate left you
  - FOR CHUCK DAMN HIM WHERE IS THAT ROBOT I NEED TO PUT LASERS ON IT RIGHT FRIGGIN' NOW
  - Wait stop

- **More deep breaths**

- **Some more deep breaths**

- **Learn some anger management techniques**
  - Creating murderous robots doesn't count
  - I mean, it kinda counts
  - Or at least it should count
  - Ask my therapist about this one

- **Get a therapist**
  - Reminder: Mad scientists aren't great therapists
  - I've been down *that* road before too
  - It's actually part of how I got here in the first place
  - Alone
  - Surrounded by murderous robots and federally sanctioned clones
  - Without Kate
  - OR CHUCK FROM ACCOUNTING, HE WAS MY FRIEND, DAMN IT HOW COULD OUR

WEEKLY D&D SESSIONS HAVE GONE SO
HORRIBLY WRONG
- Oh, the hell with it

- **Eat more cheese**
  - Like, ALL the cheese
  - Cheese is an absolute good
  - Cheese is creamy tangy forgetfulness you can buy
    by the block
  - Which I don't have to share with the robots
  - Or the clones
  - I knew it was smart to make them lactose intolerant
  - Note: this resolution may conflict with the resolu-
    tion to lose weight.

Copyright

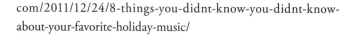